Blizzard Broth

Blizzard Broth

BARBARA GURLEY

BLIZZARD BROTH

iUniverse books may be ordered through booksellers or by contacting:

iUniverse
1663 Liberty Drive
Bloomington, IN 47403
www.iuniverse.com
1-800-Authors (1-800-288-4677)

Because of the dynamic nature of the Internet, any web addresses or links contained in this book may have changed since publication and may no longer be valid. The views expressed in this work are solely those of the author and do not necessarily reflect the views of the publisher, and the publisher hereby disclaims any responsibility for them.

Any people depicted in stock imagery provided by Thinkstock are models, and such images are being used for illustrative purposes only. Certain stock imagery © Thinkstock.

ISBN: 978-1-5320-1177-1 (sc)
ISBN: 978-1-5320-1178-8 (e)

Library of Congress Control Number: 2016920064

Print information available on the last page.

iUniverse rev. date: 12/29/2016

I'd like to thank my family and friends for all their love and support. Tracy Henry thank you for typing my handwritten manuscript! Carrie Woodard my photographer! Jean Bailie for helping read my handwritten manuscript! Facebook friends for liking my author page! Thank you God for my gift of imagination! iUniverse for all your patience and guidance! Pexels and Dreamstime for photos on my book cover!

Chapter One

Winter Ride

Roosters crow awakens Constance. Happy about bein in a warm bed in soddy. Her younger sister lay beside her, they kept each other warm. Minnesota in late November was very cold. She rose to dress and helped Gracy with her hair.

Pa was bringin in wood while Ma was cookin ham and eggs, gravy and biscuits for breakfast. Constance sat table as usual. Pa said Blessin. Ma looked tired, she was expectin her 3rd child anytime. Ma was so beautiful, a sweet smile. Constance noticed admiring looks from men at her beautiful Ma. Pa was very handsome, smart and hardworkin. A big smile always a lookin on bright side.

Pa said they would go to church, he'd get wagon ready. Ma said she felt like goin too. They all got in wagon. They could make it in about an hour. They wrapped up warmly under quilts. Singin as they went. Seemed to be gettin colder. Lots of friends and neighbors were there. Church was full on this cold Sunday.

You always arrive early Ida says. What are you doin here Elizabeth? You look pale are you well? Oh you know me I don't like to miss church said Ma. Constance Lord you are skinny as a rail! Constance looks hurt.

Preacher Sam talked bout birth of Jesus. Nice to see friends and neighbors. Constance noticed Ida leave church early. Pa went outside to get wagon, took quite a while, he had a strange look on his face. Preacher said he had announcement to make. Everyone got quiet. Friends, neighbors there is a blizzard goin on. I think we should all stay put until blizzard moves out there's plenty of firewood and food.

Pa said he felt same as preacher, I couldn't see to find my wagon. The other men agreed. Ma said she agreed would be safer to stay put. Pa tried to open door and couldn't get door open. Ida's still out there Herbert said,

Pa said sorry Herbert we are trapped in. Herbert pointed a gun at Pa and shot threw wall. Pa said we'll freeze if we open windows, you'll make all cold air come in. Pa knocked Herbert out. Ice was fallin out of the sky. No sign of Ida.

Preacher asks everyone to pray with him to keep them warm and fed until blizzard let up. After prayer men had meetin in back room. We oughta have enough food and firewood last about a week. There was canned food and meat in church cellar. At least we can stay warm and ration food. Melt ice fer drinkin water. We can make places to sleep on floor, our children can sleep together for warmth, married couples stay together, and boys can sleep in cellar. Men all agreed and shook hands.

Pa's Speech

Late at night Ma started hurtin. Pa ask for friends and neighbors attention. My woman's in a family way and friends I never thought blizzard would come. I never would brought her and two youngins out. Lord's will though I'd be need abilities of any help fer my Missus. Indian woman stepped forward I Yepa help with baby. Pa and Indian woman Yepa helped Ma walk to room where Preacher stayed. Yepa said it time baby come. Pa asked if he could help in any way. Yes boil water lots water. Pa got busy boilin water. Constance stayed by her mother's side all night. Wipin her forehead and holdin her hand.

A friend Ogin watched after Gracy. Ogin was Yepa's daughter. Ma screamed in pain. Yepa said push. Ma was sweatin this was Constance's first time to help deliver a baby. Ma fell asleep. An older woman Ann said she'd stay so Constance could get sleep, so she agreed. She hugged and kissed her Ma. I love you, Ma smiled and said I love you too.

When Constance woke up she felt rested. She ate ham and drank coffee. Went to call on her Ma. Yepa how's Ma? She rest now baby not come. Constance held her Ma's hand. Pa came in and told Yepa to get some sleep. Yepa said to come get her if baby ready to come. Pa promised her he would. Pa just held Ma's hand. Pa tell me how you met Ma, Constance said. Pa smiled and said we was all at a church gatherin, when I first laid eyes on your Ma. She was the pertiest girl I ever saw and could she ever dance! We started seein each other regular. I knew we was made fer each other. So I proposed proper like. We always thought pretty much same.

Ma woke up and said she was thirsty. Pa gave her a drink of water and broth. Pa was tellin me how he met you, you was the pertiest girl he ever laid eyes on. She smiled and said she felt same about Pa. Where's Gracy?

She is with Ms. Ogin, doin alright. Blizzards still goin glad we all stayed put.

Pa read Ma's favorite Bible verses. Philippians 4v13 "I can do all things through Christ who strengthens me". 2 Psalm 46v1 "God is our refuge and strength, a very present help in trouble".

Constance went to check on Gracy. Gracy ran to her and hugged her. Is Ma ok? Yes she's restin. Is baby here sister? Not yet Ma's tryin real hard to help bring baby. Can I see Ma? I'll ask Pa. Constance and Gracy ask Pa if Gracy could see Ma, Pa said it should be ok. Gracy gave Ma a hug and kiss. Ma said she was doin good and missed her sweet Gracy. They knelt around Ma's cot and said the Lord's prayer.

Pa ask Yepa why was taken so long for my Missus to have baby? Yepa said baby big take more time, she try but just take time. Pa said thank you fer helpin. She good woman up to Great Spirit when baby come. Pa was worn out, he needed sleep. I'll stay with Ma tonight Pa you rest.

Constance sat by her Ma late in night Ma screamed Constance jumped up. Yepa said push a big baby boy was born. Constance held her baby brother he started cryin. Yepa said to hold baby while she chewed chord, Pa held baby so Constance could help Yepa wash blood up. Yepa pushed Ma's stomach down so afterbirth came out in bucket. They washed baby and gave him to Ma to see. He's beautiful Ma said. Your Ma and me are namin our first son Wayne after my Pa. Constance stayed with her Ma while she rested.

Pa came in mornin to check on Ma. Ma smiled, Constance went for a somethin to eat. Five days still couldn't get door open. At least they could get warm and a little broth. Yepa said to boiled meat to make broth, so everyone could drink three cups a day and melt ice for water. An elderly woman was sick and weak. Women were feedin her and tryin to keep her warm. Pa announced baby Wayne was born and doin good and Ma was restin gettin her strength back.

The older woman passed away in the night, the men carried her up to the loft until blizzard was over then they would bury her.

Men have meetin. To stay alive in this cold blizzard we have to ration more. They agreed to ration what was left of the food.

People were tryin to keep warm and pass time, they read Bible in day and turned in early to save lanterns. The Preacher prayed for them to be rescued soon, for warmth and enough food. The Children played games, sang and stayed quiet. Men talked, John said we are runnin out water, food and fire wood Preacher prayed.

Ma was weaker baby Wayne was cryin more, he was hungry and Ma wasn't gettin enough milk. Pa stayed with Ma to keep her warm. They prayed for Ma to get stronger.

Preacher announced they still had plenty of broth and water. Not to fret over food. They would not be able to burn as much wood though. He said at night everyone should sleep in cellar for warmth and to save on wood. Pa carried Ma, Constance carried baby Wayne and held Gracy's hand to cellar. At least they were warmer.

Chapter Two

Lastin Hug

Pa prayed for them to be saved, he prayed they would be blessed with warmth and food. Ma opened her eyes so Pa, Constance and Gracie said the Lord's prayer for her they held hands Ma smiled and drifted off to heaven. Pa hugged her and said goodbye. Constance cried and hugged her Ma. Gracy hugged her Ma Gracy was too young to understand. Preacher came in and prayed for Ma. Everyone was sad and quiet rest of the day.

Constance was heartbroken so close to her Ma. Ma always had so much patience with her. She taught her to sew, cook, dry fruit for winter herbs that were medicinal. Ma knew all about homemade cures. And now she knew about them too. All 17 years of Constance life had been happy because of how kind and helpful her Ma was. She jumped when baby Wayne cried. He was hungry, what to do now Ma was gone. No milk for baby Wayne to drink. Yepa said I take baby. Constance gave baby to Yepa. She followed Yepa she gave baby Wayne to a young girl.

Yepa said you feed baby? She nodded. A miracle baby Wayne was nursin on her milk. Thank you God for savin Wayne. Yepa smiled her baby die she still have milk. Constance smiled. Yepa thank God for you and hugged her. Constance hugged the young mother. Maime was girl's name. At least baby Wayne would stay alive and sleep better. He stopped cryin altogether and smiled. Maime brought Wayne back to Constance at least I have a baby to hold now helps me to pass the time and miss my baby girl so. God Bless you Constance said. Why don't you stay here and you could hold Wayne anytime you want. I'll go tell Pa and Ma where I'll be. So Maime moved over closer so did her Ma and Pa. At least they were company to Constance, Gracy and Pa. They rested well that night. People prayed to be rescued no more food. Constance heard Wayne cry Maime got him and began nursin him.

Day nine Indians dance and pray to Great Spirit. A loud noise woke Constance, she could see Pa holdin somethin Pa yelled a snake! Astida used a pick to get a hole through roof, so he dropped a snake in. A tiny whole in roof we've been saved praise God! said Pa. He hugged Constance. Astida got hole big enough to drop a rabbit. Astida kept choppin ice. Astida slid through hole. Are you ok Pa ask. I Astida, Pa hugs him. Yepa my mother and Ogin my sister.

They are here and safe. Pa took Astida to them. They hug him. They try to open door. Astida shoved door open. People were weak, hungry and cold. Astida and men got fire goin. Fixed rabbits for them.

Next day people were much better and stronger people could go home. After warmer weather they had services for people who died. Ma's service also. Pa read Ma's favorite Bible Verses.

Constance takes care of baby Wayne and Gracy after losin Ma Constance tried to do everythin her Ma did. Constance favorite Bible verse helped her heart not to hurt so much. PS34 V 18.

"The Lord is near unto them that are of a broken heart and saveth such as be of a contrite spirit". Lord please help Pa to heal he is so down and out over losin Ma. Pa had been plowin from sun up til sun down he looked worn out.

That night supper table Pa said Blessin followed with good news. Grandpa and Grandma were on their way from Ireland to stay with them and help Constance look after Gracy and Wayne. Pa was in good spirits they should be here sometime in March.

Constance was happy to hear her grandparents would be lots of help to her and Pa. She knew Pa was workin too hard all day plowin and tryin to get ready for next winter took every warm day they had.

Gracy was growin fast, Constance was makin her a dress somethin to wear to school and a dress to wear to Church. She missed her Ma's beautiful sewin Ma could make anythin they needed. Also for Pa. Baby clothes for Gracy. Wayne was growin out of his baby clothes. Constance would make clothes for him to wear next winter. Thankful for Grandma on her way. Pa said he'd take her to buy material and supplies soon. She was makin a list of all she would need.

Constance did well in school she'd planned to go to college before losin her Ma. She helped doc James a few times in summer. She may be able to help him after grandparents arrive. There was so much for her to do. Gracy and Wayne were near her all the time. Gracy ask where is Ma and Constance would say Ma's in heaven. Gracy looked sad but didn't ask as often. Wayne was a good baby smiled a lot. Sometimes he'd call her Mama. Wayne loved Pa he'd say DaDa. Pa was happy when holdin Wayne they bonded. Constance rose early to fix breakfast and feed Wayne he was eatin scrambled eggs and soft foods now, She usually had breakfast and Pa's lunch ready at night Pa was always gone before first light. After breakfast and dishes were done Constance would dress Gracy and Wayne warmly and go out to milk cows and feed chickens. Gracy would feed chickens while she milked their two cows. Today Constance would make butter. She enjoyed makin butter. She also hoped to finish Gracy's dress. Pa said they may go to church Sunday so she needed to have a dress for Gracy to wear. She was busy milkin cow when she hear horses she looked out door and saw two men get off their horses. Wayne began to cry Constance picked him up and held him close to her, Gracy ran to her side. The two men walked to barn where she was. They took their hats off and said howdy Mam we been ridin a long way and sure could use a meal would be much obliged to you. Constance remembered what Pa said about helpin friends and neighbors out. My Pa'll be here any time now I reckon he won't mind if I fix you somethin. You can wash up I'll go in and start supper for Pa.

Constance has a strange feelin about them. She put Wayne in crib for his nap. Gracy stayed by her side. Constance was fixin ham potatoes and green beans. She knew Pa'd be home about sun down.

One of men said when do we eat and they started laughin. We can wait til Pa gets home but yall can help yourself to our food. Thank you Mam Constance left kitchen. Two men filled their plates full and sat at their table eatin and drinkin looked like whiskey. They were laughin and gettin louder. Baby Wayne started to cry. Shut that kid up! He's just a baby Constance said! The man walked over to close she could smell the whiskey he snickered and said where's his Pa? Pa's plowin he'll be home anytime now. I thought you was his Ma he touched her face, Constance turned away from him. He grabbed her chin you think your high and mighty don't you girl? Leave her alone Ron she'll start cryin we don't need no trouble. Constance heard a horse she saw Astida ride up. Ron said who's the Ingine? My friend. Let's just invite him in little gal. Constance went to door.

Is Seth here he held up a couple of rabbits. She shook her head no he'll be here anytime though. Ok I wait. Ask him in Ron stuck his gun in Constance's back she jerked do it or I'll shoot you. Your obliged to wait in here til Pa gets here Astida nods yes. He walks in and he shoves Constance outta way and points his gun at Astida come in Ingine! Give them to Don he'll take care of them! Sit down girl you and your lil kin wait in the barn I'll be there soon as I'm finished here. Don't hurt him he's a good friend! Go!! Ron yelled. Tremblin Constance takes Gracy and baby Wayne to barn.

God help Astida those men are mean especially Ron! She heard a gunshot! Oh God help me!

Astida was carryin his knife he got his knife outta his boot threw it at Ron his gun went off Astida lunged for Ron and grabbed his gun and knocked him out Ron shot Astida in his arm Astida shot back Constance grabbed a pitch fork ran to help Astida was at the door had been shot. Are you ok? They not ok he said. Don woke and said don't shoot! Pa rode up. Constance said Pa Astida was tryin to help and they shot him. Don said you stinkin Ingine you killed my brother Ron! He runs at Astida and Pa knocked him out cold! Oh Pa Constance runs to him and he hugs her it's ok sister you are one brave girl. Constance pulls herself together Pa thank you! I'll go get Wayne and Gracy from barn then I'll tend to his wound. You go ahead I'll tie him up and handle rest then. I'll take both into Sheriff. Constance put baby into his crib and Gracy stayed close to her baby brother.

Constance washed and wrapped Astida's arm she was thankful the wound wasn't too deep. You brave said Astida so are you you saved us from those two bad guys! She went to tend supper. Warmed beans and tators. Astida ate very little and went to sleep. Constance was so tired she tried to stay up for Pa but fell asleep. Pa got back late saw Constance asleep in rockin chair he carried her to her cot and kissed her goodnight later baby cried Pa picked him up and rocked him back to sleep.

Next mornin Pa took them to Sheriff. Pa explained what had happened. Sheriff believed Pa. Pa said Astida was at his house Constance was seein about his gunshot wound. Sheriff said he may need to question Astida and Constance. Pa said that was ok with him. Sheriff said he would keep Don in jail to charge him attempted murder. They shook hands and Pa left for home.

Astida was gone when Constance woke up. So she fixed breakfast and fed baby and dressed Gracy. Someone was knockin at the door, Constance open door and there was her grandparents they hugged what a pleasant surprise said Constance! We just got into town a fellow said he was headed this way and offered to bring us here. I get our things said Grandpa. Grandma sat in rockin chair and held baby she was so happy to see him and have ham and eggs and fresh coffee ready for you and Grandpa said Constance. Sounds real good said Grandma. Constance helped Grandpa put their things in guestroom. Where's Seth? Pa took a bad man and his dead brother into Sheriff. Jesus are you ok Constance? Yes Grandpa our friend Astida saved us and was shot by man who died. Astida left this mornin.

Constance fixed breakfast for her grandparents.

Chapter Three

Spring Water

Pa got in late that night. He was exhausted and went straight to bed. Constance got up late to feed baby. Grandpa was in kitchen. Oh see you couldn't sleep either said Grandpa. No sir with everythin that's happened too much on my mind I suppose. Constance warmed milk while Granpa held baby. He's a biggin! Just like your Dad he weighed nearly 10 pounds when he was born always smilin and happy bout somethin. How you been farrin with your Ma gone? Hurts real bad still but I know she's in Heaven. Ma taught me so much last few month I've been so busy I don't have a lot of time to fret over losin Ma. You're a real smart and strong young lady I'm real proud of you! Your Grandma and me are here for you and your Pa, to help in any way you need us to. Thank you Grandpa I love you good night.

Next mornin Grandma had already fixed breakfast so Constance fed baby and ate breakfast. Pa and Grandpa had gone to plow. Grandma how was your trip over here from Ireland? We started out there was a lot of wind and rain, some people got sick runny noses and coughin. We stayed below where it was warmer. Around day three I was gettin my sea legs. I didn't feel so sick at my stomach. Seemed like we'd never get here. Most of our trip was good on the ship. They had tea and bread, cheese, fish mostly. Some of the passengers go so ill they passed out. Your Grandpa would go up on deck every mornin to see how everyone was. Took two months to get here.

When we arrived in Minnesota a real nice man helped us get here he said he and his family were new to this part. I am so happy you are here Constance said. I'll do the dishes and you rest. I won't argue that, I can sit and knit somethin for Wayne. Idle hands are not worth much.

Constance thought warm enough to take Gracy to spring and bathe. Days were longer and warmer. Constance let her Grandma know where she was goin. She would bring lava soap and wash her and Gracy's hair. Such a beautiful warm day. When they got to spring Gracy got in after she took everythin off Gracy got her hair wet so Constance washed Gracy's long natural curly hair. Gracy loved gettin her hair washed and play in water. Gettin darker so Constance got in after she dressed Gracy. Gracy laid down on quilt and took a nap. Constance bathed and washed her hair. Soakin up sun. She heard a noise and saw Ogin gettin in for a bath. Constance offered the lava soap, Ogin said thanks so Ogin washed her hair and bathed also. Constance heard a loud splash. Astida stood right in front of her he offered Ogin somethin to drink. Ogin drank some and handed to Constance you drink Ogin ask? So Constance took a drink, she gave back to Astida, he drank and gave to Ogin, they passed drink around til all gone. They were laughin so hard that Constance fell into Astida, he hugged her and kissed her she felt so wonderful in his arms and could feel his naked body up against hers, she was feelin great and didn't try to stop him.

She was caught in all the passion she was feelin at this moment. He cradled her and hugged her so tightly this must be how love feels she thought. She felt feelins she had never experienced before. Astida was so handsome and brave. Constance said I have to go now gettin dark, so she dressed and woke Gracy up and they started home. Astida gave her fish to take home. Constance was in shock she knew she had just had an affair with Astida, should she talk to her Grandma about what had happened, she may not understand, so Constance decided to keep it to herself and God. Pa and Grandpa were home from fields they were sittin on front porch talkin. Constance took in fish didn't stop to talk to them she took Gracy in and put her to bed. She went to kitchen to dry the dishes, Grandma had gone to bed early and baby was asleep. Constance went to bed also and right to sleep.

Constance was so busy she had no time to think about Astida. Her and Grandma were gettin ready for winter cannin and dryin food. Workin on garden pullin weeds was a never endin chore. They had canned turnips and beets. Made jam from blackberries and plums. They'd put apples out to dry for winter snacks. Soon they'd have green beans, corn and tomatoes to can also.

Constance decide to go to spring late that eve. It had been two weeks since she'd been and she needed to wash her hair and a bathe. Gracy was taken a nap so she went alone. Almost dark and full moon. Constance bathed and washed her hair rememberin Astida holdin her almost seemed like a dream. She dried her hair and heard a noise Astida jumped into spring. She almost waved then a Indian girl also jumped in they were laughin and kissin and drinkin. Then she heard a baby cry and girl brought a baby boy looked like he was six months old. Constance couldn't believe what she was seein. She fought back tears and felt a lump in her throat. She gathered her quilt and soap and ran all the way home. She was heartbroken. Constance went straight to bed. No one saw her thank God!

Next mornin at breakfast Pa said he had some real good news Sheriff Thomas had stopped by and said the two men Ron and Don was wanted for murder in Northeast part of state a reward dead or alive to whoever brought them in Pa said he was goin to town to collect the reward money. He ask what we wanted from town. Material for dresses and baby clothes said Constance. I'd like some yarn and material for a new dress also said Grandma. I want candy said Gracy. Just make a list of what all you need me to bring back said Pa. Constance and Grandma made a list. Flour, sugar, coffee, corn meal, garden seed, flower seeds, threads and needles. Grandpa wanted some new coveralls and Pa said he needed somethin for the farm. Probably buy enough to get them through the winter. Never know how bad winter will be.

The next mornin Pa and Grandpa took wagon into town they'd be back in a few days maybe even one week. Constance helped Grandma in the garden most of the day. That evenin she and Gracy were in the barn and heard someone ride up. A young man went to the door Grandma invited him in. Constance and Gracy went to see who he was. Hi I'm Jed Williams he shook Constance hand and Gracys. I'm Constance and this is my sister Gracy Gates. My folks and I just moved here a few days ago. This is the closest place to ours. Would you stay for supper Grandma ask? I thank you Mam, but I need to get back, some other time though. He started to go so Constance walked outside with him. Sure you can't stay for supper she ask him it's almost ready that's real nice of you, but I need to get back, lots to do. Some other time then maybe we'll see you Sunday when Pa and Grandpa gets back from town. I hope so Constance. Constance noticed how good lookin Jed was, probably about the same age as her, she hoped she'd see Jed again.

Next day Constance and Gracy went to pick berries by the spring. Ogin was there holdin somethin in her hands Ogin said this for you Constance put down her bucket a puppy yes she's yours to keep. Constance didn't know what to say the puppy was lickin her hands and waggin her tail. She likes you, said Ogin. I'll ask Pa if I can keep her. Come we get in water. Gracy got in so Constance got in also. The three girls played in water for hours. Laughin and havin fun. It's gettin late Gracy and I have to go so they dressed and went home carryin the sweet wolf pup with them. What do we feed her ask Gracy? Table scraps Grandma will know what to feed her.

Grandma was in the kitchen. Supper in the oven. Look what our friend Ogin gave me said Constance. Oh how cute Grandma said. I'll ask Pa about her when he gets home. She's real playful and smart. Baby Wayne woke up from his nap Constance rocked him and put him down on quilt to play with puppy. They played so cute together.

Chapter Four

Constance Falls In Love

Pa and Grandpa loaded their wagon and tied their oxen and milk cow up and started for home. They bought enough supplies to last til next spring. Christmas presents also. Pa put what was left of reward money in the bank. Enough for Constance, Gracy and Wayne to go to college he hoped. He paid off property taxes and bought farm plows, new axes and everythin they needed. He would give Astida some of the money also. He saved his children.

They could see their farm through the midst. Trip didn't seem to take as long as they had thought. They found lots of bargains money went further than they expected.

The dogs welcomed them home Gracy announced Pa and Grandpa are home, she ran to them and hugged and kissed Pa. I missed you! Constance, baby and Grandma came out to hug them. They could see the wagon was loaded with supplies for winter. Pa said we'll tend to horses and get wagon unloaded then well be in to talk about our trip. Pa, Maime, her folks and new neighbor will be here tonight for supper about four thirty. We should have plenty of time to unload and wash up fore they get here Pa said.

Grandma was thrilled with her material and yarns. Constance loved the material and Gracy love her candy and wagon. She could ride baby Wayne and new puppy in. Pa picked up puppy where'd she come from? Our friend Ogin gave her to me if it's ok with you Pa. We'll see if she tames down or not before I make my final decision. We've been callin her Summer. She has such light green eyes. She friendly and playful company for baby Wayne. Grandpa had a surprise for Grandma. Her own rockin chair Grandma was so happy she left her other one in Ireland. She gave Grandpa a great big hug and kiss.

Constance just got bread out of the oven when she heard knock on door. Grandpa opened door Jed and his parents were there Grandpa invited them in. Constance went to meet Jed's parents pleased to make your acquaintance, said Constance. Pa is settin up tables and chairs in back under shade tree. Jed and his Pa went to help. Could I help you Mrs. Williams ask? If you like we could take lemonade and tea out now, so they took drinks and glasses outside they set a pitcher of each in a tub of cold spring water. The men were grateful for cold drinks. Maime and her Pa, Ma and little brother just arrived. Constance and Mrs. Williams brought out more food green beans, bread, corn, tomatoes and Pa had smoked a hog to go with their meal. Grandma baked apple pies and chocolate cake. Mrs. Williams brought watermelon, Maime and her folks brought fresh strawberries.

Pa ask people to gather around he said Blessin and people started fillin their plates a beautiful day. They had plenty of food to eat. Kids played games while men talked the women visited all afternoon. Looked like rain so they brought food inside. Constance went back to make sure they got everythin started to pour down. Jed grabbed her hand and they ran into the barn, to get out of hail. They could hear hail hittin the roof. I hope everyone is inside she said. I didn't see anyone else said Jed. Thanks for savin me she said she looked into his pretty eyes he kissed her she knew she should pull away but she didn't they climbed to the loft and kept kissin. She couldn't make herself stop him she was likin his kisses. His hands were all over and undressin her. Before she realized they were both naked. She was in love again with Jed she didn't want this moment to end.

Constance heard rain stop so she dressed and so did Jed. Jed looked at her and said I love you this was my first time. Constance said I love you too. Fixin her hair she said lets go before they miss us.

Constance wasn't feelin well she had been vomitin every mornin for a week. Grandma thought she had a virus. She was ok after she threw up. Couldn't figure why she kept throwin up in the mornins. Oh she couldn't be pregnant? She was always on time. She knew she had been late and hadn't started for two months. Oh Lord she prayed she wasn't expectin. What would Pa say? Grandpa and Grandma? What would Jed think of her? She decided not to think about this anymore. For now it was her secret, hers and Gods.

Constance was goin to wear her new dress her Grandma had made for her to wear for fourth of July. They were goin to spend the day in town and have picnic and a dance. Constance hadn't seen Jed for a month she hoped he'd be there. Pa drove them into town a hot day at least wind was blowin. Grandma stayed home with baby. Gracy looked so cute in her new dress. Smilin and happy about fourth of July party. Town was filled with neighbors and friends. There were games and lots of food. Pa and Grandpa left to visit their friends they said to meet at wagon at 8 p.m. Pa gave Constance ten dollars to spend on her and Gracy. Thanks Pa.

Constance knew for sure she'd get Grandma and baby Wayne a gift. The men were havin contest arm wrestlin she couldn't believe Astida was arm wrestlin Jed. So she and Gracy watched looked like Astida was winnin then all of a sudden Jed put Astida's arm down. Jed saw them and walked over to Constance smilin at them. How you doin Constance? Good real good blushin a little. I want to ride balloon said Gracy. Well when balloons lands you can ride it Gracy. We can walk around til then. They got somethin to drink and some popcorn. Jed showed them around. They went to store and Constance bought Grandma a set of mirror, comb and brush and baby Wayne a rockin horse. More material for herself and yarn. She bought Jed a handkerchief he liked to wear them around his neck. Also Christmas gifts, Pa would'nt go to town until after winter. Jed carried all she bought and put everythin in their wagon. She still had four dollars left Gracy could ride balloon for twenty five cents. Let's eat Constance said I'll buy your lunch Jed much obliged he said. There were hamburgers, hot dogs, bbq sandwiches, fried potatoes, mashed potatoes, slaw, potato salad, pies, cakes, brownies, lemonade, tea and pop. Jed chose hamburger, fried potatoes, slaw, potato salad and apple pie, Constance chose bbq sandwich, slaw, fried potatoes, peach cobbler. Gracy chose hamburger, mashed potatoes, slaw, peach cobbler, they all drank lemonade. They all sat on a quilt and ate their lunch. That was delicious said Jed, yes sure was! Gracy needed to go to the bathroom so they found the outhouse. People were dancin Jed ask her to dance to song Buffalo Gal.

Balloon's back said Jed. Gracy smiled and clapped her hands. Constance paid the man Gracy was the last one he could get on, Maime and Pa were goin also. Gracy waived bye to them. The hot air balloon lifted almost out of sight. Constance and Jed went to get lemonade. They had time to walk around. Jed threw darts and popped all of them he won a doll he gave to

Constance. Ok thank you Jed and hugged him. Constance knew she loved Jed and he loved her.

The balloon was back. Gracy was thrilled about ridin the balloon! Jed looked at his watch he kept in his pocket 8:30. I'll go see what's keepin Grandpa Seth said. Ok Pa we'll wait for you at our wagon. Time seemed to fly by already gettin dark thankful for the full moon. Pa came back your Grandpa is in the doctor's office he had passed out and some men brought him to the doctor. The doctor wants him to stay and rest for a few days so the doc can keep a close eye on him. I'll stay and watch Grandpa said Seth. Jed could you take the girls home? Sure can much obliged to you Jed.

Was dark when they got home. They told Grandma that Pa stayed with Grandpa. Grandma took the news pretty good. Constance helped Jed unload the wagon. Jed kissed her good night. I'll plow tomorrow for Seth said Jed.

Next mornin Constance took Jed breakfast and lunch ham, biscuits, cheese, fried chicken and apple pie with tea to drink. They sat on quilt while Jed ate ham and biscuits. Thank you for bringin the food just what I needed. Why don't you stay for supper and your welcome to stay in the barn. Is that alright with your Grandma? She's the one who suggested it. I'll go home and let my folks know where I'll be. Great that's settled then. We are so thankful for your help Jed! Breakfast and lunch will be in the oven every mornin for you so just stop by before you start to work. Supper will be in the oven for you also. That's the least we can do you are really helpin Pa and our and Grandpa. My pleasure your Pa has some mighty good oxen's the soil is easy to work with. Constance wanted to stay but she needed to get back to her chores she kissed him.

Constance helped Grandma with cannin the rest of the day. Tomorrow they'd make butter and cheese. They had so much to do to prepare for winter. She thanked God for Jed and prayed Grandpa would be well and come home.

September friends and neighbors got together at the Gates' home for gettin hogs ready for winter. They would work all day, the women set up a table with food and drinks, held hands prayed everyone ate breakfast then started to work. Grandpa still needed to stay at doctors a friend told them he'd seen Pa and went to see Grandpa. Grandma missed him even though she never said so.

The men made an assembly line like the last years when they butchered the hogs. Nothin went to waste women had an assembly line also. They washed and salted some parts. They had 40 hogs to butcher. They would leave a hog or two at preachers in case of another bad winter. Constance was grateful for Maime, Yepa and Ogins' help they were such great workers together! A wagon pulled up Grandma ran to see Pa and Grandpa. She hugged and kissed Grandpa. Constance hugged her Pa. Gracy ran up to Pa. Baby Wayne was on porch with Summer playin Pa picked up baby huggin him. Constance hugged Grandpa and said she was happy he was home they'd really missed him. Grandpa sat in rocker on porch Grandma brought him tea and somethin to eat ham and homemade bread and apple pie. Wayne stayed by his side the rest of the day.

Pa went to help the men with the hogs. Nearly dark people were leavin. Constance hugged Yepa. Ogin put her hand on Constance stomach be there baby and smiled Constance hugged Ogin tryin not to cry. Constance knew she was startin to show. Ogin was the first person to say anythin about her baby. Constance hugged Maime and said thank you for all your help. Maime stopped by to see baby Wayne real often. Just stop by anytime she said baby Wayne loves to see you. Pa said he'd take Maime home. Thanks Pa. Can I go Pa? Gracy I need your help. Ok I'll stay and help sister said Gracy. Maime and her folks lived about thirty minutes away. She could see Maime and Pa were gettin closer. Pa was a little happier. Mamie was very pretty and sweet she was good for Pa.

Chapter Five

Weddin

Jed had been stayin in their barn helpin Pa with plowin. They worked every day all day. Up before dawn and home after dark. Constance didn't see Jed much or Pa. Constance and Grandma were busy gettin ready for Maime and Pa's weddin on Sunday night after Church. Grandma had made Maime's dress beautiful white lace. Constance would be her maid of honor and Ogin her bridesmaid Constance made her and Ogin's dresses and Grandma made Gracy's dress. Maime's little brother would carry the ring. Grandpa would watch baby Wayne. Jed was best man and Maime's cousin would walk with Ogin. Pa had smoked a hog. They would go to church early to set up tables for food and drinks. Jed's Mom was makin weddin cake and homemade ice cream. Pa s' smile on his face showed how happy he was. He told Constance he'd never love Maime the way he'd loved Ma but they got along and loved each other. I love you Pa and want you to be happy. Maime's the prettiest girl I know. She's my friend and I love her too! I know Ma would want you to be happy.

The rest of the day everyone was busy but happy bout Pa and Maime's weddin. Pa and Jed got home early Saturday to get ready for Sunday. Thankful for the warm day Constance got lava soap and quilt and went to spring to wash her hair and bathe for tomorrow. She washed her long dark hair and bathed gettin darker she was about to get out of the water when she heard a splash. Jed stood up. She put her hand over her mouth. Looks like we both had the same idea he said smilin at Constance so she handed him the lava soap. He said much obliged and ducked under the water. He gave her back her soap. She threw it and it landed on her quilt. She could feel Jed's body up against her. He kissed her and carried her to her quilt. She really did love Jed and didn't try to stop him. He made her feel loved and beautiful. Dark now Constance could see because of the full moon. I love you Jed said I love you Jed. They walked home holdin hands.

Pa and Grandpa left at dawn Sunday mornin. Jed got wagon ready for Constance, Gracy, Grandma and baby Wayne to leave by seven in the mornin. They had lots to do before weddin. Church would start at ten. Constance and Jed unloaded the wagon. Then they went to church. The weddin would start at noon. The Preacher told everyone to stay seated for Seth Gates and Maime Jones' weddin.

The music started Mr. Jones walked Maime in slowly. Pa, Jed and John were already at the altar. Maime kissed her Pa and he sat down by his wife. Constance and Ogin stood by Maime. She looked so lovely in her weddin dress. Pa looked so happy! Jed looked so handsome standin by Pa. I now pronounce you man and wife you may kiss the bride. Everyone clapped for them. Preacher announced the reception would be next.

Pa and Maime cut their cake and opened some gifts. The band played for them and they danced. Constance danced with her Pa. Jed ask her to dance so she said yes. The music was to a slow song so they danced close. People were beginnin to fill their plates for lunch. Pa and Maime were gettin in Pa's wagon to go to Rochester for their honeymoon. Everyone waved goodbye. They'd be gone a week.

Constance and Jed loaded the leftover food and started for home. Almost dark when they reached home. They were tired. Jed and Constance unloaded wagon and Jed took care of the horses. Gracy and baby Wayne went straight to bed. Grandma and Constance put food away. Grandpa went to bed also. Constance went to sit on the porch. Jed was in the barn takin care of the horses. So much had happened in the last year. Trapped in the church, losin Ma, Grandpa at the Doctors. Now she was expectin her first baby. Did Jed suspect. What did he think of her. He told her he loved her and she'd told him she loved him, more than once. He never mentioned marriage though. Jed was goin to stay in the barn and plow while Pa was on his honeymoon.

A wagon pulled up a young man and woman. They walked to porch howdy my name's Zack and this is my Missus Jean we're travelin west. Nice to meet you I'm Constance and I'm Jed they shook hands. We need a place to stay Jean's expectin our first born. Constance offered the barn loft. Jed could sleep in Pa's room. Much obliged Zack said. I'll let Grandparents know you are here. Jed could you show them where to put their horses? Be glad to! Jed led the way to the barn.

Grandma and Constance fixed a meal for Zack and Jean glad for leftovers from weddin. Jean and Zack sat down blessed their food and ate. They didn't talk very much. Grandma went to bed Constance put food away after they ate. Late at night Jed woke Constance up Zack says his Missus is hurtin real bad. I'll go see about her said Constance. She fixed her hair and put her robe on and went to see about Jean. Constance climbed to loft Jean was moanin in pain. I hurt real bad said Jean. I'll stay with you Jean Constance said. Jed climbed up to loft do you need anythin? Yes I need hot water a string and lots of clean rags. Or you stay here and I'll go get them I know where everythin is. Constance ran in and grabbed everythin and put water on to boil Grandma got up and Constance told her Jean is in labor. I'll watch water thanks Constance grabbed her apron and knife and ran to loft.

Constance said Grandmas boilin water send Zack after it ok he said. Jean are you ok? For now Jean said. I need to check you I think you are in labor. I think so too Jean said. Can you stand up so I can help you change. I'll try she said. Jean stood while Constance put a old gown on her so she wouldn't mess her gown up. Constance helped Jean lay down and get comfortable. Constance prayed for God to guide her. Baby Wayne was the only baby she'd ever helped deliver. Jean screamed. My first baby and don't know what to do said Jean. I know what to do when you have pain push and the baby will come out. Ok I'll push, so the next pain Jean pushed. Constance could feel the baby's head. Good girl Jean I see baby's head just push when you feel pain. Jean screamed and baby was almost out Constance pulled the baby out. A boy Constance said. She gave him to Jean he's not breathin Jean said so Constance turned him upside down and spanked his bottom he cried out thank God. She handed him to Jean. Thank you Constance and God. Jed brought hot water. Constance put butcher knife in. Tied strings got knife out and cut cord in middle. She needed to ask Ogin what to do next. Oh I need bucket Zack handed Jed a bucket. Constance pressed Jean's stomach and afterbirth came out. Jed could you go get Yepa and Ogin for me? Sure I'll go now. She washed up and washed baby. For now they were ok baby was nursin.

Nearly Dawn when Constance went to sleep. Grandma went to see about Jean and her baby. Jean was nursin him, she said they were ok. Ogin climbed ladder Grandma said she would be in the house if they needed her. I'm Ogin Constance friend nice to meet you Ogin. I check you ok? Ok Constance said you would. Ogin looked at Jeans stomach and pressed down. Ok Ogin said good you look good. I look at baby Ogin looked at his fingers and toes and stomach he look good too she gave him back to Jean thanks he's my first baby. You do good you rest. Ogin climbed back down. Constance wants to see you Ogin ok I go to Constance. Ogin knocked on the door Grandma said come in Ogin. I'll go get Constance for you. Constance Ogin's here tell I'll be right there. Constance tidied her hair and put on her dress. Ogin how are you? Good let's eat some breakfast. There was ham and biscuits coffee and milk and gravy. Ogin was very hungry she ate all her food and Constance gave her food to take with her. How's Jean and her baby? They both look good. Everythin happened so fast. Jed helped some. Good I go now bad snow come you bring woman and baby in. Ok. Is Yepa and your family ok? Yes they good. We have food Grandma gave Ogin a sack some canned goods, butter and ham. Constance gave Ogin a homemade scarf to wear they hugged Ogin and said see you soon.

Grandma Ogin said a bad snow storm is on the way to bring Jean and her baby in. I'll send Jed and Zack to bring her in. Jean slowly climbed down the ladder. Zack carried baby down. Jed told them they could stay in the house a storm was on the way. Jean and Zack stayed in Pa's room for now. They'd have some privacy. Jed and Zack went to see about horses and cows fed them and shut barn door for warmth. Jed and Zack brought in wood and more meat from the smoke house. Before a snow Pa would leave extra feed for livestock sometimes snow was so deep they couldn't get out to feed the animals. The rest of the day they prepared for the storm.

Snow blew in that night eight inches of deep snow still snowin that mornin. Thankful for wood and food. Jed couldn't open the front door. Grandpa figured Pa and Maime would stay put until they could travel. Constance hoped he was right. The soddy was full of people every one tried to look on the bright side. Snowed all day. After super the men played cards. Gracy and baby Wayne played hide and seek. Jean nursed her baby. Grandma and Constance washed dishes. Made preparations for tomorrow's meals. Grandma sat in rockin chair and knitted. Constance put baby Wayne and Gracy to bed. She was tired so she said good night.

Chapter Six

Trapped In

Two weeks and they were still snowed in. They had plenty to eat, drink and were warm. A lot to be thankful for. Constance and Grandma decided to try and fix a Thankgivin dinner. They could have ham, sweet potatoes, green beans, corn, bread, apple, pumpkin, peach pies and chocolate cake. They'd miss Pa and Maime for sure. They could have food all ready by Thanksgivin Day.

Jean said she would make a chocolate cake. Grandma got the ham in the oven. Constance made the pies. Grandma baked bread. The women worked all day and night gettin all the food ready. Gracy licked the spoons. The women were up early they fixed breakfast. Put the bread in the oven, they could eat at noon. Constance washed dishes so Grandma could go freshen up. Constance changed Gracy's dress and fixed her hair, she changed Wayne's diaper and clothes also. Constance changed and freshened up.

Everyone gathered round table. Grandpa said the Blessin. We pray for Pa and Maime to come home as soon as they could. Grandpa cut up the ham then passed it around. Everythin looked and tasted delicious. Everyone was in good spirits. After the meal Jed helped Constance wash dishes and put away the food. Constance missed her Ma this was the first Thanksgivin without her. Jed was talkin but she didn't hear what he said. What? I just said this was a wonderful Thanksgivin yes it has been. We are warm, safe and full of good food. I miss my Ma, she could cook anythin, she taught me all she knew. I have been blessed to have had such a patient lovin mother. I wish I could've met your ma said Jed. She would've liked you. And I would have liked her too. How bout a game of checkers? Sounds good Constance went to get them. They sat at the kitchen table. Played til after midnight. Still snowin.

December first still snowed in. They had to ration food and wood. They couldn't get door open snow was so deep. Everyone tried to make the best of their situation. They heard a loud sound the front door opened and Astida walked in. Jed shook Astida's hand. God Bless you man! Astida had food in a sack. Rabbits and squirrels. Grandma and Constance started preparin their meal. Jed, Zack and Astida went to see about the animals. Constance and Grandma fixed rabbit stew. They had onions, potatoes, carrots and tomatoes to add to the meat. So grateful they had run out of meat a couple of days ago. Jed and Astida went to smoke house and brought in more meat.

The livestock is all ok said Jed. We fed them and left extra feed in case we get more snow in the night. The stew was ready they blessed food thanked God for it then ate. Sure was delicious, Zack said. Astida left early in the mornin no more snow in the night. The next few days the sun melted the snow. They were able to take care of livestock and feed them better. A calf was just born so they had to keep inside so it wouldn't freeze.

Jed and Constance went to look for Pa and Maime. They rode horses. The snow was almost gone. They rode into town and ask if anyone had seen Pa and Maime. The man at the Inn said they did stay there they'd just gotten married. They left after one week. Should have gotten home by now. Constance was nearly in tears. Thank you Jed said. Constance they must be at a farm between here and home. We'll stop at every farm on our way home I know we'll find them.

First farm a man answered the door he said he hadn't seen anyone that fit their description. So Jed and Constance rode to the next farm, then the next one was abandoned. We better stay here tonight it's gettin dark, we have a long way to go. Ok sounds good. Jed put their horses in the barn. Constance lit the lantern and gathered wood to build a fire. Jed brought wood in. Constance warmed up ham and coffee. Constance and Jed slept close to fire and each other. They were awakened late. A loud moo a cow and her calf were in the back part of soddy. Jed tried to open the door but couldn't he could see a blizzard blowin in Ogin was runnin to the door so Jed opened the window and Ogin climbed in. She was nearly frozen. Constance and Jed hugged her and tried to warm her. Ogin was warmin up. Constance wrapped quilts around Ogin. Ogin fell asleep. Jed found more firewood in the soddy, stacked against the wall that saved their lives.

Now that he could see better the cow was a milk cow. They could live on cow's milk and water. Thank God! No tellin how long they would be trapped in. Jed had given the horses extra feed he prayed it was enough to keep them alive.

Next mornin Jed built fire and they had milk for breakfast. Constance and Jed looked around for any canned or dried food. Behind a curtain was a cellar sweet potatoes, green beans, corn and turnips. This food would save them.

Chapter Seven

Christy

Ogin was gettin stronger. Constance gave her milk three times a day. Ogin was sittin up and walkin some. Three days still couldn't open the door. Would they be trapped here at Christmas? Constance prayed they wouldn't. Ogin put her hand on Constance's stomach she smiled you good now. Thank you Ogin you're an angel. Jed was milkin the cow. He had found a bucket, Constance washed it out real good, the milk was delicious kept them from starvation. Jed held her at night and kissed her til they both fell asleep.

Constance woke up in pain oh no is it time God? Another pain she screamed are you ok Constance ask Jed? I don't know. Ogin was there I help now. What can I do to help ask Jed. You boil water, find string. Jed went to build a fire to boil water in a pan he'd found he washed the pan then put ice from the window to boil. The snow was so thick outside. He could hear Constance scream. She's havin a baby was it his?

Ogin said push Constance had said that before so she tried her best. Thinkin about her Ma dyin givin life to baby Wayne, would she die too? Oh God I pray for strength to live and raise my baby. Constance screamed and pushed Ogin pulled the baby out, good baby here. Ogin tied strings, baby cried Jed ran in Ogin gave baby to Constance and chewed chord in two. Baby was cryin Ogin press on her stomach afterbirth came out. Constance cuddled her baby. A girl! Ogin washed baby with some rags an gave her to Constance to nurse. She's beautiful said Constance! Jed said yes she is!

Jed ask Ogin what to do next? She need rest and to keep warm. Jed kept fire goin. Ogin made a place by fire for Constance and her baby girl. They piled all the quilts and buffalo hides they found in soddy on Constance and baby girl. Ogin made a gown and diapers for baby she found some material, scissors and needles and thread. She made several gowns and diapers. Constance rested for hours. When she woke her baby was cryin. So Constance nursed her until she was content. Then she burped her. You good? Ogin was standin over her smilin. Yes thank you so much Ogin you are such a angel, you hungry? Yes I could drink some milk. The milk was warm and good Constance drank all of it. She was gettin stronger a good sign. She new what she would name her baby since she was born December twentieth Constance would name her Christy Elizabeth. After Christmas and her Ma.

Jed brought her more milk. Christy Elizabeth said Constance. That's a real pretty name Jed said. She has your blue eyes he said and dark hair. Christy smiled she was so good and easy to love!

Thankful for the wood, milk and food. Four days calf died. Christmas Eve. Jed and Ogin were preparin the calf for Christmas meal. They would have beef, sweet potatoes, corn, turnips, milk for desert canned peaches. Grateful to be warm, safe and full tummy's.

Christmas day Constance and Ogin prepared their meal. The soddy had lots of supplies to cook with. She hoped all her family was safe and warm. Jed was keepin the fire goin and holdin Christy. The window opened and Astida and a Indian girl with a baby boy about two years old climbed in. My people die cold no food we walk long way see smoke from chimney. Ogin hugged Astida and ask about their mom Astida said she go to Great Spirit. Ogin cried Constance hugged her.

Astida, his wife White Doe and son Bear warmed up by fire. Ogin brought them milk. They all drank the milk. The Christmas meal almost ready. They could hear ice hittin the roof. Constance said dinner is ready they held hands Jed said Blessin grateful for warmth, food and good friends and family. They ate slowly. Bear was feelin better he was smilin and eatin his food. Constance wished them all a Merry Christmas. Constance and Ogin cleaned up dishes. White Doe held Christy.

Constance sang O' Little Town of Bethlehem for Christmas. Ogin sang a cute song in her language. They all sat around the fire grateful for one another and the soddy. Whoever lived here was prepared for winter. They had food and firewood to last til spring if they weren't rescued before winter was over.

Christy was cryin and runnin a fever. Constance got up to try and rock her to sleep, hopin she didn't wake the others. She put a wet cloth on baby's forehead. Ogin came into see about her baby. She too hot said Ogin. Ogin wet more cloths and wrapped Christy in them. Christy went to sleep.

Next mornin Christy's fever had broken. Constance nursed her. Baby went back to sleep. Jed built fire. Constance wrapped Christy in quilts and lay her by fire to keep her warm. Bear stayed close to Christy to watch her.

Grandma was fixin breakfast she prayed every day for Seth, Maime, Jed and Constance to return home safe. Christmas was lonely and quiet this year. Grandpa and Zack kept fire goin. They had been trapped in nine days now. So much snow and ice. Jean and her baby were doin good. Gracy ask about Constance and Pa often. Grandma would say they'll be home as soon as snow melts.

The men talked or played checkers, cards or dominoes. The women talked, cooked, sewed, knitted. Grandma and Jean were makin a quilt to pass the time. Jean said she and Zack met, fell in love and got married. Jean was workin in the store when she met Zack. They went to church together to picnics also. Zack had no family and Jean only had her Pa who had a drinkin problem. Her and Zack were on their own. Grandma said they could stay here and Zack could help plow, she had plenty of room for them. Jean said she would ask Zack about stayin.

Gracy turned four Grandma and Jean made cake and they celebrated Gracy's birthday. Grandma made a new dress for Gracy. Grandpa made her angel from oak. Gracy was a happy little girl.

Chapter Eight

Runnin Out of Food

February warmer days snow was meltin. Astida was goin to go for help. He would walk to nearest farm and get help. The horses didn't survive. Jed would stay and keep wood in fire so they could stay warm, they were runnin out of food. Jed was weak, from lack of food. Astida was the strongest so he wanted to go for help. White Doe fixed food and milk to take with him. They prayed for Astida to make it safely to find help.

Cow didn't have much milk nothin to feed her. Jed found her dead next mornin. Jed, Ogin and Constance prepared the beef. They boiled some of it. Grateful for meat and broth. They all ate slowly. They were all weak the beef might save them.

Astida walked all day he was freezin cold he look up and saw smoke. Hopin a farm. He walked towards the smoke he saw a soddy. A man walked out to the barn. Astida handed him a note that said "My name is Jed Williams we are trapped in soddy three women and two year old boy and a two month old baby girl. Astida is tryin to find help. God Bless You. Jed Williams".

The man said come in and get warm. I'm John this is my wife Faith. Faith fixed Astida some beans and milk. I'll hitch up the wagon will go help your friends. Faith fixed food for them and they left to go help.

Almost dark Astida pointed to soddy. John pulled up as close as he could. Astida went in first they were all sittin by fire White Doe ran to Astida. I'm John he shook Jed's hand. God Bless You. They decided to leave first light. They were so happy to be saved.

They all got in the wagon after the supplies were loaded. Will be at my place in no time John said. They were freezin but happy cuddled close for warmth. They could see the smoke in soddy. Faith opened the door and they all went in. John put horses and wagon up.

Faith had beans and stew. They held hands and Jed blessed their food. After meal, Constance and Ogin helped Faith with the dishes. So nice to have company said Faith. John and I have been trapped in all winter. Seems all we do is keep fire goin eat and sleep. And in the summer we work every day to prepare for winter. That's true Constance said. Jed and I went to look for my Pa and Maime they had just gotten married and went on their honeymoon in Rochester. The man at the Inn said they had left. We stopped at a couple of farms, but no one had seen them. Then we stayed at the soddy and got trapped in from snow and ice. Sounds like you've been through a lot. You make yourself at home we have room for you to stay as long as you need to. If it's ok we are tired sure we have a loft you can rest up there it's warm too. So Constance, Ogin, White Doe, Bear and Christy climbed loft to rest. Jed and Astida stayed below on cots by fire so they could keep the fire goin all night.

Constance didn't wake up all night baby slept all night too on her neck. Constance woke up to the smell of bacon and biscuits. She felt rested. She fed Christy. Ogin and White Doe woke up. Bear was still sleepin. So warm up there she would cover Christy and let her stay warm. White Doe woke Bear. He got on her back and she carried him down the ladder. The men had gone out to check the animals.

Constance helped Faith in the kitchen. After she slept good and ate she felt stronger. She knew she was very skinny. Constance scrambled eggs. Ogin put wood in the fire. White Doe watched after Bear. He had more energy than anyone. Constance heard Christy cry so she went to loft to see about her. She was wet. Constance changed her. She would wash clothes today. After breakfast everyone sat around fire and visited. Still wasn't safe to travel snowin again.

The men had brought more food and wood in. John couldn't get the door open so Astida climbed out the window. He handed John's wood and meat as long as he could ice was fallen from the sky. Astida climbed back in while he still could.

Trapped in again. Faith was so sweet and helpful she shared anythin they needed. John said they should wait to make sure blizzards was over before anyone tried to go anywhere, men had died close to their front door when blizzards hits they couldn't see and the temperature drops so fast way below zero. You are right said Jed thank you for sharin your home with us. My Pa and Ma always helped people when you help someone someday somebody will help you. While the men talked Constance took a nap in the loft with her baby.

Ogin and White Doe helped Faith with supper. Beans, cornbread, peach cobbler, coffee and tea. Everythin was delicious Jed said. Constance and Ogin did the dishes.

Faith had their soddy fixed up real cute. Red curtains and rugs. This was the biggest soddy Constance had ever seen. The loft was roomy also. Gettin stronger from eatin better. Was she imaginin that Jed was avoidin her. He was keepin his distance from her baby too. Did he know who Christy's dad was? She was so brown, dark hair and blue eyes. She saw Astida lookin at Christy. White Doe was actin different too. White Doe was expectin a baby not sure how far along she was. Bear had so much energy he played and laughed a lot.

Faith loved to rock Christy. She had lost a baby a miscarriage. Constance didn't mind she could see Faith needed to hold and rock her baby. Anytime she needed to be changed Faith would change her. Constance could cook or wash clothes.

Chapter Nine

Warmer Days

Time seemed to fly. Already three weeks had gone by. The snow was beginnin to melt. Jed and Astida were goin to go to let Grandpa and family know we were safe and see if they were ok. They packed up supplies, food and water for a few days. Jed and Astida would bring a wagon back to get them. They all joined hands and prayed for Jed and Astida to have a safe journey and return as soon as possible. They hugged one another. Constance hugged Jed. Prayin for his safety. The weather would still get bad, snow and blizzards had happened in March before.

Almost dark Jed saw smoke from a soddy he knew it was his folks place. Pa was in the barn. He hugged Jed Thank God your home! Your Ma'll be so happy! He shook Astida's hand let's go tell your Ma your home. Mrs. Williams was thrilled to see her son! She fixed a meal for them.

After dinner Jed told them all about what had happened. How he and Constance found a soddy to stay in with Ogin they were Blessed with cow and calf and firewood. How Astida and White Doe had found them and stayed with them. How John and Faith had let them stay with them. Constance her baby, Ogin, White Doe and Bear were there now. That's a miracle the way all you kids have survived this freezin cold winter. I know you're weary so you can rest anytime you like tomorrow you and Astida can take my wagon and bring everyone here. I'll ride over and let Constance family know she's safe and on her way here. Thanks Pa said Jed. That's a great idea. Mrs. Williams prepared food for them to take.

First light Jed and Astida went to get everyone. Mr. Williams left to go let Constance's family know she was safe. About a hour Mr. Williams arrived Grandpa was in the barn milkin the cow. Hello Mr. Williams said Grandpa. I've got wonderful news my son Jed and Astida are on their way to get Constance, Ogin and White Doe they are all safe. Grandpa was so happy to hear Constance was alive. Thank you for the great news Jim. Please come in. Jim went into their soddy. Grandpa announced she's alive! Constance is on her way home with Jed and Ogin and a few others. Saints be praised said Grandma. Constance is safe said Gracy. Baby Wayne clapped his hands and smiled. Mr. Williams stayed rested had lunch and coffee. They were in good spirits. He offered to go look for Pa and Maime in spring. Much obliged said Grandpa, soon as Jed and Constance are home will talk about goin to look for Seth and Maime.

Constance, baby, Ogin and White Doe and Bear gathered all supplies thanked Faith and John for sharin their home and food with them. John offered Astida a job so he talked to White Doe and Astida said yes. John said they could stay with him and Faith in the summer they would add on to their soddy for Astida and his family. Constance Ogin and Jed said goodbye. To Astida and White Doe, Ogin said she'd be there when time baby and hugged her. Happy to be goin home to Grandma, Grandpa, Gracy and baby Wayne. Home was on Constance's mind.

Constance could see smoke from soddy she couldn't wait almost there. Summer was outside now she was really growin! She started barkin. Grandpa opened the door and ran to greet them and Gracy ran out, so did Grandma, Zack, Jean and baby Wayne, Constance hugged them all. Gracy hugged I missed you! We better go in your cold said Gracy so they all went in. Christy started to cry so Constance took her to be nursed. Ogin stayed by Constance. Gracy sat by Constance is this my baby sister she ask. This is your niece her name is Christy. She's pretty said Gracy can I hold her? After she nurses you can hold her dear. Baby Wayne walked in he wanted to get in Constance's lap so she let Gracy held Christy in the rocker. Constance set baby Wayne on her lap and hugged and kissed him. I sure did miss you baby Wayne. Love you baby Wayne said. They cuddled for a while. Felt so good to be home. Christy was asleep so Constance put her on the bed. I'll stay and watch her said Gracy. Baby Wayne said I stay. Ok come get me if she cries. I will said Gracy.

Ogin and Grandma were fixin supper. Grandpa, Jed and Zack were in the barn. Jean was changin her baby. So Constance sat the table. Grandma wasn't talkin too much she had a lot on her mind. Still worried about Pa and Maime still no word from them. Ogin went to get the men for supper. Grandpa said the blessin everythin was delicious. Jed was fillin them in on being trapped. Constance and Ogin clean dishes and table, Grandma prepared breakfast and for Grandpa, Jed and Zack they would start plowin in the mornin,

She's cryin said Gracy so Constance went to see about Christy. She needed to be changed. Constance changed her. Constance went to soak the dirty diaper. Gracy was so helpful. Baby Wayne was so watchful of Christy. She wash diaper and hung it up to dry by the stove.

Next mornin Jed, Zack and Grandpa left to start plowin. They were gone til dark.

Jed and John were goin to look for Pa and Maime in the mornin. Constance went to feed chickens and gather eggs. Jed walked into the barn. Thanks for goin to look for Pa and Maime said Constance. I know he'd do the same for me he said. Jed closed the barn door. I need to talk to you Constance. Let's go to the loft she said more private up there. So they climbed up ladder to loft. What's on your mind? You said Jed I want to ask you a real important question. Ask then. We are a lot alike we should be together married, I want to marry you he kissed her yes I'll marry you Jed. When I get back we can get married I love you Jed. I'll go feed Christy then meet you back here Constance said I was thinkin the same thing too! Constance took eggs and went to nurse her baby. She nursed Christy changed her, checked Gracy and baby Wayne.

Jed was already in the loft when she got there. She undressed and got under quilt. They talked all night about their future. I'll miss you she said, not as much as I'm goin to miss you. Promise me somethin said Constance. You come home before winter. I promise. God keep you safe. Grandpa, Constance, Grandma, Gracy, Zack, Jean, baby Wayne and Summer all said goodbye to Jed and John.

Grandpa and Zack left for fields. The women worked in their garden, served, cooked and visited the rest of the day. Zack and Grandpa would be home at dark. Late at night a knock on door, Grandpa let Astida in he had White Doe and Bear with him. White Doe was in labor. Grandma boiled water, Constance and Ogin helped White Doe get comfortable. Grandma brought rags, string, knife and bucket. Constance helped White Doe change her gown. Jean stayed with baby Wayne, Christy, Bear and her baby. I'm goin to check you White Doe said Constance. She couldn't feel the head. Ogin checked her also. White Doe screamed Constance said for her to push I am goin to check you again said Constance she prayed for God to guide her hands. She could feel baby's head with feet first she knew she needed to turn the baby around so she pulled the baby's head around. White Doe screamed the head of the baby came out. Thank you God! Constance held baby and swatted her bottom a cry! Ogin cleaned up Constance washed baby and gave her to White Doe.

Constance told Astida White Doe had a baby girl so he went into see her. Constance went right to sleep.

Net mornin Constance changed and nursed Christy. She went to see about White Doe. White Doe was ok and her baby was nursin. Thank you Lord. Grandma had breakfast ready for her. She heard Christy cry so Grandma went to see about her. Constance ate slowly grateful White Doe and her baby were alright.

Chapter Ten

Pa & Maime

Zack got wagon ready for church a nice warm Sunday in May. The wagon was loaded they all went. Nice to see friends and neighbors after the bad winter they'd had. The Preacher prayed for Pa and Maime to be found and for Jed and John to be safe. Are there any announcements? Constance stood up I have announcement to make. I'm goin to be married to Jed Williams when he gets home from lookin for Maime and Pa and you are all invited! Christy started cryin so she sat down. Thank you Miss Constance. They sang "May the Circle Be Unbroken". Such a beautiful day People visited while the woman prepared lunch, ham, green beans, potatoes, gravy homemade, bread, chocolate cake and apple pie. Coffee and tea. After everyone ate all the women cleaned and put dishes away. Preacher Sam said any time they wanted they could fix lunch after church.

Next mornin Grandpa and Zack went to plow. Astida, White Doe and Bear and baby girl left. Faith was alone so they wanted to go as soon as White Doe could travel. White Doe named her baby Yepa after Astida's mother. Constance would never forget how Yepa tried to save her Ma. Yepa was a special and beautiful lady she missed her so much her heart broke for Ogin, Astida and White Doe. She understood how they missed their beloved mother. Say hello to Faith for me said Constance White Doe nodded yes. Ogin went with them to help White Doe and her baby. I see you all at church or anytime you need me I am here for you love you all and God Bless You. Constance, Grandma, Jean, Gracy, baby Wayne waved goodbye to them.

Let's sit on the porch and drink tea said Constance. So Constance went to get glasses and tea. Grandma, Jean, Gracy and baby Wayne sat on porch and drank tea and ate a cookie. So much had happened they needed a treat and one another's company. Funny thing happens for a reason said

Grandma. Summer was lickin baby Wayne she was so tame for a wolf. Gracy ran and played with baby Wayne they all laughed and enjoyed one another's company. We work hard we deserve to play hard said Constance. Jean said that's so true! The days were gettin longer so they could work in the evenin after supper. When weather was nice they could cook outside and eat outside under the elm tree.

Jed and John had been gone about two months. Grandpa and Zack worked every day plowin the fields. Constance, Grandma and Jean stayed busy in the garden. Now they were cannin green beans, corn, tomatoes, onions and peppers. They would build a fire outside in the evenin and can food for winter. The garden was doin real well this year. So much to be thankful for!

Sunday Zack and Grandpa took them to church they all looked good so warm today. They prayed for Jed and John to return safely. Such a beautiful day they had lunch after church. Nice to have fresh vegetables from garden. Pastor Sam smoked a calf for lunch and the women cooked potatoes, made a garden salad and cookies for desert.

Children played. Men talked. Women visited. Lots of laughter and fun.

Around seven p.m. they all left for home. Constance was thinkin about Jed. She needed to start preparin for their weddin. What would she wear? She'd talk to Grandma and Jean for ideas on what to wear. The most important thought was prayers that Pa and Maime were safe and Jed and John were on their way back home with Pa and Maime. Grandma and Jean could start makin her dress, Gracy's, Ogin and Jean's dresses. Then they'd make Jed, Grandpa and Zack's shirts. She prayed that her Pa would be there to walk her down the aisle. Almost home now. She'd start plans tomorrow.

Jed and John stopped at every farm no one had seen Seth or Maime. Most people didn't think they were still alive due to the snow and freezin winter. They decided to stay in an abandoned soddy. They built a fire so they could see and warmed up some of the beans and ham. Sure was good. They ate and went to sleep.

Jed didn't get much rest. He got up and built a fire fixed coffee. He looked around soddy in back corner again and were two bodies under a quilt. Oh God no it was Seth and Maime they were holdin hands. He covered them up. He told John he'd found them both together John went to look. At least we know they are in heaven John said.

Will take their bodies back to church will bury them there. Sunday preacher Sam can pray for Seth and Maime and family. Jed, John and pastor Sam buried Seth and Maime at church cemetery. They placed a cross on the graves. Preacher prayed for them. John went home Jed thanked him for all his help.

Summer was barkin Constance was workin in the garden she saw Jed. She ran to him and hugged and kissed. So grateful to God you are home. Good to be home he said. I'll go put horses up. Ok then will sit under shade tree and talk. Constance got some tea and sandwiches for them. Jed's home she said. Grandma looked worried. I'll let you know what Jed found out about Pa and Maime somethin told her it would be bad news. She sat down and got tea ready and handed Jed a glass of tea thank you. He drank tea prayin for the right words. You must be worn out Jed. I am tired. Did anyone see Pa or Maime? He held her hand. We stopped at every place we saw and no one knew anythin about them. We stayed in an abandoned soddy, this hurts like hell to have to tell you this. Even if its bad news at least we can have peace of mind said Constance. They're not comin home are they? They died didn't they Jed said yes they are gone. Constance cried in Jed's arms. I'll go tell Grandma she said you can rest in the loft Jed.

Grandma, I already know said Grandma quietly. I pray they didn't suffer in the freezin cold winter and hungry for food. They cried and hugged. When Grandpa got home Jed told him the sad news. I figured they tried to make it home before the blizzard said Grandpa. The whole family includin Jean and Zack were down and out over Pa and Maime.

Sunday people gathered around graves. Preacher prayed. Constance and Gracy put flowers on the graves. Last winter was one of the worst anyone had ever seen. The preacher invited everyone to stay and have lunch. The women fixed some ham and potatoes, cabbage and turnips and fresh tomatoes.

Men sat together talkin about gettin crops ready. Children ate fast so they could play together. Faith was so nice to them she really cheered Constance and Grandma up by talkin about her plans for women workin together on quilts and clothes for winter. Faith before winter why don't you and John stay with us we have room we could share our food and wood. Winters are so terrible here we would all be safer to stay together in the winters. That's a great idea Faith said. I'll ask John. If John agrees we could pack our food, wood, quilts and bring our milk cows and chickens. Til winter's over. I'm all for it too said Grandma. Maybe the next winter you could all stay with us said Faith. Great idea Faith said Constance. Jed's folks should come too we could make it through the winter a lot better stayin together said Constance.

People started to leave, Constance and Grandma thanked preacher for kind words of Pa and Maime. They loaded wagon with leftover food. We'll be back in a couple of weeks Jed said. Look forward to it said preacher. Christy started cryin she was hungry. Constance nursed her. A sad day no one talked all the way home.

Nearly dark when they got home. They all were tired helped unload the wagon and said goodnight.

Chapter Eleven

Constance and Jed's Weddin

Constance took Christy, Gracy and baby Wayne to spring to bathe and play in the water Baby Wayne loved the water. Constance filled a bucket of water to warm for Christy to bathe in. Constance washed Gracy and Baby Wayne's hair. While they played she washed her hair and bathed. She was almost finished when she heard Christy cry oh God no a wolf was growlin at Christy. Constance ran out of the water to try to save her baby girl. She jumped between Christy and wolf and covered Christy's body. She heard the wolf growl when she looked Summer was fightin the wolf thank you Lord for Summer. Gracy and Baby Wayne were in the water they ran to Constance. Summer killed the wolf. Constance hugged Summer and gave her a slice of ham. Summer was very beautiful almost two years old very strong and protective of them. She stayed near Gracy and Baby Wayne.

Constance bathed Christy and let her sit in the bucket of warm water, she smiled and patted the water. She heard a splash. Jed jumped in. You gettin in Constance? So she jumped in the water and they talked and kissed while kids played in the water. Constance told him about the wolf how Summer killed it. He said he'd go look to make sure the wolf didn't have rabies. It was gettin dark so Constance dressed while Jed looked at the wolf. They walked home together. He said wolf looked ok no rabies.

Grandpa met them your Grandma isn't doin well. I need to get her to a doctor. I'll help you said Jed. So they helped Grandma get in the back of wagon and off they went to the Dr. Constance prayed she would be ok. Constance got supper for her family. Jean helped her. She put Gracy, Baby Wayne and Christy to bed early. Poor Grandma she always worked so hard maybe that's why she wasn't feelin well. She worked from sun up til sundown. So much to do to prepare for winter. Jean was a lot of help. Tomorrow after breakfast they would work in garden and make butter, jelly and green beans outdoors under shade tree while children played and napped. Gracy could feed chickens. Zack could work in the fields.

Constance and Jean worked all day they got everythin done in one day. They would work every day until Grandma got home. Zack got home after dark so he would eat supper then take care of horses, then go right to bed. His days were long he plowed all day. Late at night Constance heard a knock on the door she opened the door John and Faith, Astida, White Doe, Ogin, Bear and baby were there because their home burnt to the ground. You are welcome to stay with us. So Constance got quilts and pillows for her friends.

Next mornin John, Astida and Zack left at dawn to plow. Faith told them how the wind blew and fire spread through the soddy and barn. They tried to put fire out but the wind was too strong they lost everythin they had except horses, ox and chickens. Constance hugged Faith while she cried. God will see us through said Constance. We can close in the lean-tos and add a loft with a door from our soddy into lean-to. Then we can make barn larger for livestock before winter. With your chickens and ox we'll have more meat this winter. Faith nodded in agreement.

That night a baby ox was born. Constance took Gracy and baby Wayne out to see him. He was so cute. Baby Wayne pet and hugged the baby ox. Summer didn't know how to handle baby Wayne givin his attention to the new ox, Summer sniffed the ox and licked baby Wayne's face they were all happy about the baby ox.

Next day Gracy, Baby Wayne and Bear stayed in the barn with baby ox most of the day. The women worked in the garden preparin for winter. John came home early to work on soddy extra room for winter. Faith was in better spirits losin everythin in the fire had her down and out. So everyone worked together they got so much done.

The next month went by so fast. No word from Jed or Grandpa about Grandma. John was finished workin and expandin soddy and barn. They would have a lot more room for winter. The children could sleep in the loft. Couples could sleep together. Ogin and Constance could sleep in the loft also. Astida and White Doe could stay in add on with Zack and Jean. They had enough beds and quilts to keep them warm.

Constance heard a horse good it was Jed and she ran to hug and kiss him. How's Grandma? Doctor said she needs to take it easy she has a heart problem, your Grandpa's goin to stay with her til it's ok for her to come home. I'll fix you somethin to eat I know your plum tuckered out. Zack and Astida walked up and shook Jed's hand. Constance went in to fix Jed a ham sandwich. Jed sat and told about how Grandma was just tired and not much strength. Grandpa was stayin at boardin house to be close he stayed with her most of the day.

Jed and men went to work at dawn. They would work til sunset. Women worked cooked and served til dark. Kids played with baby ox all day. This evenin the women would make butter.

July seemed to fly by. Constance and Jed to get married Sunday after church they would spend their honeymoon in Rochester and visit Grandma and Grandpa. There was so much to do to prepare for the weddin. All the dresses were ready. The men's shirts were almost finished. Gracy would be flower girl, baby Wayne would carry the ring he was almost three years old. Ogin was her maid of honor. Zack was Jed's best man. Jed's father would give her away. Faith said she'd love to watch Christy for her while she was on her honeymoon. Christy was so good for Faith. There would be lots of food for all the friends and neighbors.

Saturday night Constance dreamed of her Ma huggin her and sayin she was so very proud of her. Pa hugged her and said he loved her and they all three held hands and laughed together. Constance woke up she had tears in her eyes she missed her Ma and Pa but she knew they were in heaven and would be at her weddin in her heart. She went back to sleep.

Constance was awake before she heard rooster crow. Faith and Jean had breakfast ready so much to do before her weddin today. She thought about the dream she had about her Ma and Pa their love was with her. As soon as she ate breakfast she would get ready to go early she would dress at church. John would take them to church. Jed, Zack and Astida had already left earlier. They loaded wagon with food and trunk with their clothes. What a beautiful day for your weddin said Faith I agree Constance smiled.

You look beautiful Faith took Constance's picture. Thank you Faith, I'm so nervous prayin everythin is right. It will be smiled Faith and she hugged Constance. Mr. Williams walked Constance down the aisle. Jed was so handsome she really loved him. The preacher said you may kiss the bride. Constance was in a daze she hoped she said I do. Jed kissed her a long time she heard people laugh and clap. Preacher announced food and cake at their reception. They ate lunch and cake. They opened gifts. Jed thanked everyone for attendin their weddin.

Three men rode up on white horses. Jed, John and Zack walked over to them howdy said Jed. The men said they were there to arrest Astida for stealin a horse. You know what the punishment is for a horse thief said the man. Astida aint a horse thief you're burnin daylight and you're not takin Astida anywhere said Jed. Well then we'll just hang him here then. The men was gettin louder Constance and women took all children into the church. Constance told the children to lay down in the floor she heard a gunshot she looked out the window oh no Jed was shot the men hand cuffed Astida. The preacher ran out to see about Jed. The men put a rope around a tree limb and made Astida get on a horse. Constance saw Zack take out his gun Summer jumped on one of the men. Zack aimed and shot and fell to ground, he was shot too. Constance grabbed a gun and went out to help. She pointed the gun at the men drop your guns! Now! The men laughed and said no aint lettin no skinny bitch woman tell me what to do he pointed his gun at her so she shot and he fell down the other man drew to shoot so she aimed and shot he fell down too. White Doe came out go cut rope off Astida Constance said. White Doe ran to help Astida. Constance ran to help Jed, Jean ran to help Zack.

God please guide me Constance, Faith and Ogin began tryin to save Jed he had a bullet lodged in his chest Jed was unconscious at least he wouldn't feel any pain. Jean boiled water Constance sterilized the knife. She began the bullet was deep so she ask for men to turn Jed over thank God the bullet was out! Faith cleaned wound and stitched up wound.

Zack's wound was right side of his heart Constance prayed Zack screamed out in pain so Astida and John held him down Astida gave Zack a drink of fire water. He was more calm. Astida let Zack drink all he wanted after he was ready Constance began. Thank you Lord for guidin my hands. Constance reached the bullet and removed it quickly. Zack was calm and almost asleep. Faith and Ogin cleaned his wound and stitched him up. Constance washed her hands and went to see about her husband. Everythin happened so fast she was married to Jed Williams she was Constance Williams.

Jed was sleepin she kissed him and held his hand. Gracy and baby Wayne hugged her and Summer was by his side. Mrs. Williams came in and told her Jim and John had gone into town to let sheriff know what had happened they took the three men in. One had died and the other two were wounded. You are so brave said Hope you think and react so quickly you saved Astida's life and protected our children. I prayed for help and God helped me I was so afraid but God gave me courage and strength to pull the trigger. Jed and Zack were so brave and ready to defend Astida they risk their lives. I'm so happy to have married your son Jed they hugged.

Jed slept rest of the day next mornin Zack was sittin up ready for breakfast. Jed woke up and Constance gave him some broth. He needed rest to recover from bein shot. John and Jim got back and they said they would take Jed and Zack to Jim's place much closer than the Gates' farm. Constance, White Doe, Jean and Faith rode in back of the wagon. Astida, Bear and John rode horses to Jed's folk's. The children rode in the covered wagon driven by preacher Sam.

Jed was gettin stronger so he stood up to walk but couldn't feel his feet so he sat down in rockin chair. Constance hugged him and said he would heal in time when he was ready they would try again. Baby Wayne laid his head on Jed's lap and Summer licked his face. Gracy hugged Jed and said I love you Dad. Jed just smiled.

John, Astida and Jim went to Gates' to plow and feed animals. White Doe, Ogin and Faith went to cook and take care of garden they took Bear and their baby girl. They would stay until Jed and Zack could come home. Hope and Constance and Jean would take care of Jed and Zack. They would help Hope to prepare for winter. Jed needed somethin to do with his hands, so he sat on the porch and whittled, Zack was gettin stronger so he and Jean gathered wood and garden vegetables, fed animals, milked cows.

Jim and Astida came by to let them know Grandpa and Grandma had got home yesterday late in the day. Constance ask Jed if she could go see them and he said he'd be ok if she went. Constance got her things packed along with Gracy, Christy and baby Wayne. They were so excited about seein Grandparents! Hope and Jean would be there for Jed and Zack. Summer had puppies in the night. She would stay also.

John drove them home in the wagon. He was such a nice man and so helpful. When they got home Grandma was sittin on the porch with Grandpa. Constance, Gracy and baby Wayne ran to hug Grandma and Grandpa. Oh we missed you said Grandma. Gracy, baby Wayne hugged them Grandma sat down to hold Christy. This is where doctor told me to spend time on porch to stay cool not to work too hard. Then that's what you should do said Constance. Everyone stayed close to Grandma the rest of the day. Grandma had lost some weight she was pretty thin. Grandpa was lookin good just tired. He was very carin of Grandma he loved to be home. Grandpa always took care of his family. If he wasn't plowin, gatherin crops he was cuttin wood or fixin somethin around their home. In the winter Grandpa kept fire goin or brought in wood. In winter he made furniture, rockin chairs or wood boxes. Sometimes he played checkers or cards to pass time.

Constance would stay a couple of days, she wanted to be with Jed. He was always on her mind. They would have to wait to go on their honeymoon til Jed was well enough. They might spend the winter with Jed's parents. Hope already ask her and Jed to stay through the winter. She'd miss Grandma and Grandpa and her home, but Jed came first. Thankful for Ogin, Faith and White Doe stayin to look after Grandma. Before winter she'd send one of Summer's puppies to protect Bear and grow up on the farm. Grandpa, John and Astida could work together to take care of crops and animals, cuttin enough wood for the winter. If Jed could travel they would all come before winter to smoke the hogs. Constance and Jean work well together along with Hope. Zack was healin fast and worked well with Jim and great company to Jed. Hope wanted one of Summer's puppies also, so they needed to find homes for two of the puppies. Gracy and baby Wayne wanted to keep them all. They loved animals. Baby Wayne missed his baby ox he and Gracy stayed in the barn most of the day.

Chapter Twelve

Locusts

Next mornin Constance woke to sound of bell cover everythin all food in the house said Grandpa locusts are here! Constance put a sheet over Gracy, baby Wayne and Christy, stay here and cover up until I come and get you she told Gracy. Faith, Ogin, White Doe and Grandma were coverin the food puttin lids on everythin. Constance shut the windows and front door and ran outside, locusts were everywhere they sky was black. John, Astida and Grandpa were tryin to fight them off. Constance ran to the barn to shut the door. Locusts were in the trees and on the corn crops. Constance swatted the locusts that were in the barn. She had never seen so many the inside of the barn was filled with them. She felt as though she should stay in the barn and fight the locusts and protect the cows and horses they were all over the four sheep. Constance tried to get locusts off them but couldn't she was so exhausted she'd been fightin locusts for hours. She prayed for her family and their crops to be ok. She had almost killed all the ones in the barn. Oh no the sheep's wool was gone! The quilt was gone and handle off pitch fork and shovel were gone. She looked out the window gobs of locust still out here. The men were still fightin locusts. She ran outside to help fight locust she couldn't see. Grandpa shoved her into the barn stay he said so she did what he told her.

When she woke up she looked out the window daylight. She saw the destruction the locusts had done. They had eaten the leaves, fence, wagon, crops. She ran to the soddy Faith hugged her are you alright? Yes I stayed in the barn all night. Gracy and baby Wayne ran to hug her. So thankful they were ok. Grandma said they ate her rockin chair and most of food and wheat. The soddy smelled like locusts. I'll go see about Grandpa Constance ran to the field to see Grandpa, Astida and John exhausted from the locusts. She hugged Grandpa. The locust had destroyed all the crops.

Workin together to fix all the locusts had destroyed would take a lot of hard work and time. Constance couldn't take her children back to Jed because locusts had eaten the wagon. So John and her would go on horses to see about Jed and the others. They would leave first light. Ogin, White Doe and Faith worked cleanin the soddy. The only food left was what they had canned. They still had two milk cows, chickens and hogs to butcher. The winters could last up to five months. John and Grandpa would make a trip into town before winter to get supplies for winter.

Constance kissed her children and hugged everyone before gettin on the horse to go. Hard to do but she knew she needed to go see about Jed and the other people at the Williams' place. They arrived around noon. The place looked like theirs, locusts had been here too. Jim and Zack were out in the barn. Constance ran to see Jed he was on the porch. They hugged and kissed. Damn locusts said Jed I was no help. Jed it's ok. No it's not. I just sat in this chair and did nothin! There was nothin anyone could do the locusts ate everythin no one could stop them. They ate our wagon, Grandma's rockin chair, the wool off the sheep and our food. There was too many to fight. Jed looked sad. Jim and Zack walked up. I never seen so many before said Jim. Me either John agreed. Looks like there were more locusts here than at the Gates' place. They were in the house before I could shut windows and doors said Hope. I'll help you said Constance and she hugged Hope. We can go into town before winter and buy supplies. Jed and I'll build a wagon. You can stay at our place through winter said Constance, we are low on firewood too, we can bring your wood and food so we will all stay warmer and not run out of food, we don't want to put anyone out said Jim. We would all be better off if we stay together. We can get ready to go in a couple of weeks. Then Grandpa and John can to town for supplies. The rest of us can butcher and smoke the hogs. So Jim and Faith agreed to stay with the Gates' through winter. The next day Zack and Jed worked on makin a wagon. Constance, Jean and Hope cleaned locusts out of the soddy. By dark Jed and Zack had finished makin the wagon the locusts didn't eat the wheels, so they could leave as soon as everyone was ready to go.

Jed tried to walk every day but he couldn't feel his feet, he could stand up but not walk. Jim and John helped Jed anytime he needed anythin at all. Jed was doin better makin the wagon had helped him have self-worth.

He was smilin more. Constance was relieved to see Jed in better spirits. Jim and John got all livestock ready to go. Two oxen, twelve chickens and two extra horses, four hogs, Summer and her four puppies. Hope had all her trunks ready, quilts, beds, all he canned food. Locusts had hit so hard there wasn't much to load. They were ready to go. The trip home would take longer with the animals tied onto back of the wagon. They traveled most of the day before they reached the Gates' place. Grandpa came to welcome them home. They all hugged Gracy and baby Wayne came runnin out to greet them. So wonderful to see them! Ogin brought Christy out. Christy smiled and hugged her mom. Faith brought some tea out for everyone. She was always so thoughtful of others. Grandma was takin a nap. Faith and Ogin fixed supper, beans and cornbread. They were all quiet disbelief of all that they had survived the last four years. Nice to just rest with family and friends.

Next day they went into church. Friends and neighbors were exchangin stories about the locusts. A man stood up and told how about ten years ago the locusts swarmed by the millions they ate trees and made the water turn brown couldn't drink the water. The livestock ate the locusts and the milk and meat was ruined. People were so hungry they ate the dead locusts, was the worst he'd seen of them. Grandpa stood up and told how locusts had ruined crops, food and ate the wool off the sheep. He invited all to come out and help butcher the hogs. Grandpa said seven families would stay together this winter to survive the blizzards and what the locusts had destroyed crops and food. After church other families talked about stayin together for warmth and food for winter. A very great day they would see friends next Saturday to prepared meat for winter. They made it home before dark.

They all worked every day gettin ready for winter and for Saturday. The women cleaned soddy and worked makin butter and cheese. The food would keep them alive. Ham, canned vegetables, green beans, corn, turnips, carrots, beans, onion, sweet potatoes. Blackberry jam, plum jam and strawberry jam. Grandma was helpin to figure out what they would need from town to survive the winter. So far, flour, sugar, coffee, tea, salt, pepper, material, thread, needles, yarn and candy for children. They could survive on water gravy so flour was very important. Bein trapped in and not able to get the meat, gravy kept them alive.

Saturday people arrived first light. The women had breakfast ready. Ham, gravy and biscuits. They had ten hogs and over one hundred people to share with. Grandpa figured each farm would get two hogs for five farms each farm would have twenty people to feed. The men also would hunt deer and buffalo in October. Jed was a great hunter he usually brought deer and buffalo home. Astida and Zack would hunt also.

Constance went to bathe at the spring she went alone. She needed to be by herself. She washed her hair then dressed she felt as though someone was watchin her so she sat on her quilt to dry her hair someone moved an Indian girl very thin walked up to Constance. Constance offered her some ham and bread, the girl took it and ate hungrily. How had she lived through the winter. She was about four years old. I'm Constance she pointed to herself. The girl didn't say anythin. She smiled a little and sat down on quilt. The girl jumped in the water another little boy walked up he was about three years old so Constance offered ham and bread he ate very hungrily. Was gettin dark so Constance folded her quilt the girl and boy hugged and held her hand while they walked home. Ogin would know how to talk to the children.

Summer and her puppies ran to greet them. There were only two puppies left. The little girl and boy pet Summer and her puppies. I'll get Ogin said Grandpa. Ogin came out the little girl talked to Ogin. Her mother die she try to have baby. The little girl was takin care of her little brother they had no home or nowhere to go. Does she have any other family asked Constance. No, no one. Tell her, her and her brother can stay here Ogin told them what Constance said the girl hugged Constance. What's your name she pointed to herself and said Sutra and pointed to her brother, Nand. Constance pointed to each of them and said their names Sutra, Nand. Gracy ran up and pointed to herself, Gracy, Gracy said. Sutra, Nand Wayne pointed to himself, Wayne, Wayne said Nand. Constance took them to the kitchen. Faith fixed them some ham and gravy, green beans and for dessert chocolate cake. They ate all the food. Then Gracy took control they played on the porch with Summer and her puppies.

First light Grandpa and John went into town for supplies they'd be back in about two weeks. Grandpa still had reward money, they would be able to buy what they needed.

Chapter Thirteen

Grizzly Bear

Jed could feel his right foot so he could walk with a cane at least he could go fishin and bathe in the spring. Jed was so good to baby Wayne, little Wayne was always by Jed's side. Jed had plans to deer hunt with Zack, Grandpa, Jim, John and Astida in about three weeks middle of October. The deer and buffalo would be food for winter. For now they could fish and gather wood. They caught a lot of fish for supper. Jed was happy about the catch.

Constance, Ogin and White Doe followed Sutra to where they had lived when her mother had died. They walked for nearly two hours. Sutra pointed there behind shrubs a cave. Ogin went in first, the cave was bigger than it looked from the outside. Ogin made a fire for light. Constance looked around there was a buffalo hide, some clothin. In a corner was Sutra and Nand's mother. So sad to see her or what was left. Constance ask Ogin to tell Sutra the men would take her mother to church Sunday and they would pray for her mother to Great Sprirt, God. Sutra seemed ok with that. Constance, Ogin and White Doe gathered what they could carry, buffalo hide, clothin, feathers and beads for Sutra. The buffalo hide would be used this winter for covers on cots to keep them warm. When they were ready to go the sky was dark. They had taken longer than they thought, too dark to walk home will stay here tonight said Constance.

They sat in a circle held hands and Constance blessed their food, Lord thank you for this meal, Bless and keep us safe through the night, Amen. They ate ham, cheese and bread and drank water, they shared an oatmeal cookie. They would need food for breakfast, so they saved some ham and bread for tomorrow. Constance and Ogin spread the buffalo hide on the floor it was large enough for all of the girls to lay on. Constance dreamed about her Ma huggin her and sayin (hugs last) and she hugged her Pa they looked so beautiful. Constance woke up a loud growl oh no a grizzly bear was growlin at them. Constance told Ogin to stoke up the fire to keep him out. Constance loaded her gun she knew she better not miss he was gettin closer and closer. Stay behind me Constance said. Ogin had a fire goin better she could see better now. She said God please don't let me miss. Constance pulled trigger, he was gettin closer, she reloaded, Ogin and White Doe had a stick of fire to keep him back she was ready to shoot again he was angry and wounded oh no he had White Doe's arm, Constance grabbed a stick of fire and burn grizzlies mouth he let White Doe go he scratched Constance neck she felt pain. She backed up fired again thank God he fell to the ground! Ogin ran to Constance to see about her. Sutra cried and ran to Constance. Constance was covered in her own blood. Ogin tore off bottom of her dress and wiped her neck off. She was still bleedin. Ogin see about White Doe I'm ok. Ogin tied White Doe's arm to stop the bleedin. White Doe's wounds were deep. Constance and Ogin worked together to try and stop her bleedin. The wound was on her wrist they prayed for White Doe and Constance to heal.

White Doe went to sleep. Ogin kept fire goin Sutra also was asleep. Ogin made thread out of her dress. White Doe's wrist needed to be stitched so did Constance's neck wounds she found a needle in the cave and began to stitch White Doe's wrist. Her wrist was barely hangin on. She wrapped her wrist in part of Constance's dress. Ogin had stopped White Doe's bleedin. She began to stitch Constance wounds she had one deep wound and two smaller cuts from the grizzly bear. Constance fell asleep. She woke up to smell of food. Ogin had cooked some bear meat, smelled so good. White Doe was sittin around the fire eatin some bear. God only knows she needed to feast after her bravery and nearly losin her wrist and life.

Ogin had stayed awake all night taken care of her and White Doe, they would have died without Ogin. God Bless Ogin! Sutra was eatin beakfast. She seemed ok this mornin. Thankful she had brought her gun, her Pa said a good life saver always carry a gun. Never know when you'll need it to save a life. Constance couldn't believe how good the bear meat was! She couldn't stop eatin it! This would mean more meat for the winter! After she made herself stop eatin she looked at White Doe's wrist, swollen and red. Constance washed her wrist in hot water then covered her wrist with part of her dress material. Do you feel like walkin home? White Doe nodded yes.

They gathered what they could carry, Ogin had cooked extra bear for them to eat. They had walked about an hour White Doe needed to rest so they rested for about an hour. They heard noises. Summer ran up to Constance, so happy to see her Constance hugged her. Astida and Zack walked up. White Doe ran to Astida huggin him so happy to see him. Zack hugged Constance, Ogin and Sutra. Thank God you're here. White Doe tried to fight the grizzly bear and he nearly took her wrist off! Ogin saved us both. She kill bear big bear said Ogin. We go get bear said Astida. Yes can you make it home ask Zack? Yes we can said Constance. Here bear food you take Ogin gave Zack some of their food, they would need to eat before draggin the grizzly home. The bear would be heavy. When we get home we can send help, said Constance. Ogin told them how to find the bear. Summer went with Astida and Zack.

Finally Constance could see the soddy. Grandpa ran out to greet them, your hurt a bear a grizzly attacked White Doe let's get you in and look at your battle wounds said Grandpa. Faith and Jean cleaned her and White Doe's wounds with hot water and poured whiskey on their wounds. White Doe screamed out in pain. Ogin rubbed honey over White Doe's wrist. Faith poured whiskey on Constance neck ouch burned a lot Ogin rubbed honey didn't hurt as much. Constance was so tired she turned in early. She slept so good didn't wake up til rooster crowed.

Zack and Astida were home. They had to drag the grizzly all the way home. They were plum tuckered out. Grandpa, Jed, John and Jim took care of the bear. They were thrilled! Now they would for sure have enough food for the winter. The problem was gettin trapped in soddy and no way to get door open they couldn't get to the meat inside the soddy they'd figure somethin out. Constance was a real hero around the soddy, she'd never felt so appreciated before. Grandpa said the grizzly bear weighed nearly one thousand pounds! I knew he was huge said Constance!

Sunday all friends came out for dinner, Ogin cooked bear it was delicious! There were over two hundred people there! They just heard about Constance shootin a big grizzly figured they'd have a whing ding! They greeted everyone and shared the bear meat, green beans, mashed potatoes, gravy and strawberry cobbler with them. A lot of people said they didn't have food for winter, so Constance gave them bear meat to take home. Oh no a young expectin woman bent over in pain. Constance ran to help her. Sorry I just felt pain. Why don't you come to soddy you can rest said Constance. Faith and Ogin offered to help her also. They helped her to soddy to sit down. Faith went to get water boilin. What's your name ask Constance? Beth, Beth O'Mally, I'm sorry puttin you out, spoilin your whing ding said Beth. Don't be sorry you're no bother at all said Constance! Beth screamed out. Mind if I take a look ask Constance? Beth nodded ok. Constance washed her hands. She checked to see if she could feel the baby's head. How many babies have you had? My first one said Beth. Beth when I say push I need you to bear down. I'll try. Constance could feel baby's head Beth screamed push said Constance and baby came out! Thank you Lord! Beth was unconscious. Ogin and Faith washed baby girl while Constance tied strings and cut them. She laid baby girl on Beth.

Beth woke up oh how beautiful she kissed her baby and cuddled her. Constance was relieved she was able to help Beth. Beth was so young and tiny. Did she have family? Constance went outside Jed walked up to her and hugged her. A baby girl! A healthy baby girl. Does she have family ask Constance. All the people had gone. Guess we need to find out Jed went in followed by Constance. My name is Jed, hi I'm Beth. You live around here close by? Beth started to cry I have no one left. Constance hugged her. That's alright Beth don't worry you can stay here as long as you want you and your baby girl. Beth seemed better.

Ogin brought food for Beth. Beth ate fed her baby and went to sleep. Ogin said she'd stay with Beth and take care of her. Constance and Jed went for a walk. You know you are gifted at helpin people don't you Constance? I need to go to college to learn more, there's so much to learn. I could help so many more people if I knew how. When would you go? I'm not sure yet. Christy is almost two years old now. I'll pray about this said Constance. Somehow they ended up in barn so they climbed to the loft where passion and love for each other took over. They stayed late in the loft. Constance tidied her hair and clothes kissed Jed and went to see about Beth.

Thank you for helpin me said Beth. I'm just thankful you are both doin so good Beth. Her baby girl was nursin. Have you thought of a name? Yes after my Ma, Abigale Constance after you. I'm so honored to have your baby have my name said Constance. They hugged. I was so afraid said Beth. I lost my Ma she died her and baby brother both gone. She had no one to help her and I was too young to know what to do. My Pa was never around he drank whisky all the time, he wasn't good to Ma. She loved him though. Sorry about your Ma. I lost my Ma given life to my baby brother a Indian woman named Yepa tried to save Ma but she couldn't. I had a good Pa he had just remarried Maime just before last winter they were on their honeymoon, both were found in abandoned soddy blizzard came last winter.

They were tryin to get home. I'm sorry Beth said. The winters here are freezin cold blizzards we get trapped in when blizzard hit sometimes all winter. Thank you for lettin us stay, I can sew, work garden, cook, clean. I'll try to earn my keep said Beth. We could use the help. Grandma has to take it easy doctor told her too.

Summer was barkin someone rode up on a horse.

Chapter Fourteen

Young Couple

Grandpa was talkin to a young man. Constance walked outside. Constance this young man is lookin for a young girl named Beth. My name's Pete Beth ran off she got upset because I didn't want to get married. She's expectin a baby. Yes she is here let me see if she is ok with seein you. Wait here. He almost went in anyway but Grandpa said you can sit on the porch and wait son. Pete was all torn up over Beth he told Grandpa he needed to talk to her. As they sat on the porch snow fell.

Beth a young man is here to see you his name is Pete. Do you know him? Beth's face turned real red, yes he's my boyfriend. Everythin happened so fast. I thought he loved me and knew my baby was his, he said he wasn't sure my baby belonged to him. He's the only boy I've ever been with. I was so hurt. I just left him in town at Rochester and heard about the whing ding here so I rode in with a man and his wife and their three children. Do you want to see him? Yes I'll see him said Beth. Constance was goin to get him but he was already standin at the door, she almost bumped into him. Constance went on outside to give them some privacy. She figured they needed it. She said a prayer for them hope for the best

Grandpa was sittin on the porch so she sat by him. The snow was fallin harder the ground was already covered in snow about seven inches. Temperature had dropped a lot freezin cold. Well if it keeps this up we'll be inside for a while said Grandpa, glad we added on and made a door into the barn to check on our animals and put our food and wood in the barn for winter, we might get trapped in least we won't go hungry and cold neither will our livestock said Grandpa. Yes that will help a lot we have more room for our friends. So happy all our friends are stayin with us, now we can accommodate even more with our indoor toilet in the barn said Constance, a great invention of Jed's said Grandpa. No one will have to go out into the freezin cold anymore. We'd best be gettin out of this blizzard said Grandpa so they went in.

Well looks like we are all in for the night said Grandpa. Supper's almost ready Faith said. Smells real good said John! Constance went to see about Christy she was sittin on a quilt Gracy was watchin her. Baby Wayne was takin a nap. Sutra and Nand were nappin too. She let them be.

Next mornin Constance went to see about Beth. Mornin said Constance mornin. Pete and I are back together she had a happy smile on her face. Good how's little one doin? She nurses real good she looks just like her Daddy. He ask me to marry him this spring we don't have the date yet but you're invited. That's wonderful we can all help you out like makin your dress. That's real nice of you I'll ask Pete what he wants to do.

Guess what said Pete we can't get the door open we are all trapped in! How much snow do we have ask Constance. Not for certain he said. I'll talk to you later Beth. Constance went to look outside. All she could see was snow deep snow. With all the extra room everyone was happy the fire was goin, White Doe and Ogin kept the wood in the stove. The ham smelled good so she ate breakfast.

Constance and baby Wayne went to barn. Grandpa was standin by hole baby Wayne ran and tumbled into the hole. Oh God no! Constance covered her mouth Grandpa looked first he motioned she looked down Jed had caught baby Wayne. Whew what a relief!! Jed carried baby Wayne up rope on his back!! Baby Wayne hugged her. I fell down potty hole and they laughed. Constance and baby Wayne had gone to barn to use the necessary. This was so much better than last winter more privacy. They had two milk cows, four oxen, four horses, two sheep, ten chickens, two roosters, Summer and one of her pups. They had bear meat and hog meat and two bucks all frozen for the winter.

They had about fifty pounds of bear left. Constance had given most of the meat to people in need. Jed walked in. I wondered where you was. I was just lookin at our meat supply said Constance. First blizzard's early this year November 4, 1889, we didn't get much chance to hunt this fall, probably should start rationin our food. You are right Jed better to start early than late winters here can be brutal said Constance. At least we have all our animals inside and our food supply. We are goin to build a box around all of the meat so nothin can get to it. Good idea. If warms up and melts the snow some of the men will go huntin. I'll pray for a warm spell said Constance me too. They hugged and kissed.

Everyone got along and worked together. Constance talked to Faith, Jean, White Doe, Hope, Ogin and Beth about how to make their food supply last through the winter. We have lots of beans said Faith. We could have beans every day for one meal. We can make broth and soup on Saturday and Sunday with bear meat. Breakfast we can make ham and biscuit gravy add bits of ham to the gravy. One good blessin we have ice to melt for plenty of water. We can make pie and cake once a week for dessert. When we can get the door open we can make ice cream, said Hope. We aren't low on food now but if we don't cut back early we could be in danger of runnin out. The snow's early this year said Grandma. She had been taken a nap so Constance let her sleep. That's true said Faith. We have lots of flour and corn meal. We can make dumplins and cornbread. We have sweet potatoes, pumpkins, onion and peppers. Also green beans, turnips, corn, sauerkraut, tomatoes, beets, strawberry jelly, blackberry jam, we have a lot more food than we had last winter. We can bake lots of bread and biscuits too said Constance. I can make pumpkin pies said Beth! Great we will all work together and help each other. Let's join hands and pray. Constance prayed for strength to endure the winter for health and unity of all to keep them safe and warm Amen.

Faith and Hope worked to prepare beans, cornbread and apple pie. Beans would be their supper. Ogin and White Doe would make stew for dinner. They would add bear meat to a big pot of boilin water, onions, tomatoes, carrots, potatoes, peppers and salt. They would have stew and cornbread. Durin the week lunch would be homemade bread and gravy. Sometimes chili.

Snowed all day snow was half way up the window now. Constance walked to the barn with all the children they wanted to see the animals. Jed was feedin the animals baby Wayne wanted to help. Jed gave him the bucket to hold while the horse ate. Can I help all the time Daddy? Of course you can, me too said Bear, me too said Nand! So the next horse Bear held the bucket. Then Nand held the bucket. Looks like you've got lots of good help said Constance. Sure does! Guess will go back said Constance she kissed Jed and the three boys stayed to help Jed. Jed was so good with the boys! He wasn't as close to Gracy, Christy or Sutra.

Constance went to talk to the girls about plannin Thanksgivin dinner. They all sat at the table and talked about what they could have. We can have deer roast and ham for our meat said Faith. I can make dressin said Constance. I'll bake bread said Hope. I cook potatoes and gravy Ogin said. I cook sweet potatoes said White Doe. I'll bake a cake said Beth. I make cookies! said Gracy. I make Cookies! said Sutra. This is makin me so hungry said Constance! Me too said Gracy me too add Sutra! I'll make apple cider said Grandma. Wonderful! We can fix all desserts the day before Thanksgivin said Faith. Looks like we are goin to have a meal fit for a King said Constance.

Such a joy to be trapped in women who tried to make the best out of this situation they worked hard and respected one another. There was more people this winter but they also had more to eat! The soddy atmosphere was so cheerful such a blessin!

The men stayed busy with the livestock and bringin in firewood. Grateful for all the warmth and love they had for each other!

Chapter Fifteen

Workin Together

The day before Thanksgivin Constance made cornbread for her dressin. The soddy smelled so good! Pies and cookies in the air! Everythin should be done by noon on Thanksgivin day! Faith and Hope would cook the roast and ham early in the mornin. Gracy and Sutra had so much fun makin cookies! We are sisters said Gracy and Sutra nodded and said sisters. Baby Wayne, Bear and Nand were helpful tastin their cookies! They all agreed cookies were good.

The snow was meltin slowly but at least the men got the barn door open. They all went out to gather firewood and snow for ice cream. What a fun day! Jed, Astida and Zack went huntin in the evenin. Around four p.m. Grandpa said all the kids should go inside startin to snow again. The men had already gone for their huntin adventure. Happy about the day out of the soddy Constance and all the women cooked the rest of the day. Almost dark Constance looked out the window oh no a blizzard! Where was Jed, Zack and Astida? Constance, Ogin and White Doe and Jean went to the barn. Grandpa, Jim, John and Pete were talkin. Grandpa open the door a blizzard's goin on and see if Jed, Zack and Astida are outside, so Grandpa opened the door, no one was there. Constance was in disbelief Jed, Astida and Zack hadn't come home yet. Ice was fallin from the sky and so freezin cold out! Too dangerous to open the door again. You can go back and eat supper we will stay here and let Jed, Astida and Zack in as soon as they get home said Grandpa. I'll bring supper out to all of you said Constance.

In a daze Constance fixed beans cornbread and coffee for Grandpa, Jim, John and Pete. White Doe and Jean helped carry the food. White Doe and Jean were down and out about their men out in the blizzard. They thanked the three women for bringin out their supper at least they had a fire goin to keep them warm. The temperature was below zero. Constance and all women prayed for Jed, Zack and Astida to come home unharmed. Constance dozed off to sleep.

She woke up and went to look out window. Astida and Jed were walkin to barn deep snow where was Zack. Constance ran to the barn. Jed and Astida are outside Grandpa! White Doe and Jean ran in behind Constance. Jim, John and Pete tried to open barn door they couldn't get the door open. Snow's too deep and icy said Grandpa. Let's try front door. They all ran to the front door. The door won't budge. Grandpa got a sledge hammer and busted open the window he gave sledge hammer to Jed and said bust the door to the barn down! Jed grabbed it and went to barn he chopped on the door he gave hammer to Astida tried and broke down the door thank God! Constance hugged Jed he was so frozen! White Doe hugged Astida he was frozen also, get them in where it's warm said Grandpa! Constance, Jed, White Doe and Astida went to warm the men by the fire. They'll need a change of clothes said Constance. Faith and Hope brought dry clothes for the men they got under bear hide by the fire to warm up. Constance gave Jed hot coffee to drink. Astida drank hot coffee too! Constance and White Doe lay under the bear hide to warm Jed and Astida.

Grandpa nailed a board over the window. Jim, John and Pete worked on barn door. When Jed could speak he said Zack, Zack gone. Constance knew what Jed meant. Poor Jean she loved Zack with all her heart. I'll tell Jean said Constance.

Constance prayed for the right words to tell Jean about the loss of her beloved Zack. Jean cried and said no no it's not true he's alive I just know Zack's alive. Constance hugged her Jean I know you are hurtin he's in heaven he's not sufferin. You cry all you want, I am here for you don't worry Jean I love you we all love you, you have a home here. Jean sobbed she was very quiet all day. She was takin Zack's death really hard. Beth was tryin to keep Jean company.

Thanksgivin dinner was ready so everyone gathered around the table held hands while Grandpa said the Blessin. Lord we are grateful for family good friends a warm home and our great meal Amen. Grandpa was so tough yet so kind and thoughtful of everyone. Jean burst into tears and left the table she went to the barn. Constance and Ogin went to see about her. Jean she cryin. Constance hugged her. You are not alone Jean I'll stay with you said Constance. I go get food. I build fire said White Doe, thanks said Constance. Constance sat down by Jean while she cried. The fire felt warm it was very cold in the barn. Ogin and Faith brought food and hot tea. Jean ate a little bit she said she wasn't hungry. So Ogin put food by the fire to keep warm for them. Jean didn't want to leave the barn she found peace there. Jean dozed off to sleep Ogin and White Doe stayed with Jean. Constance went to see about Jed he was asleep by the fire so Constance stayed with him to keep him warm.

She cry for you Ogin woke Constance early in the mornin. Ok I'll go to her. Constance and Ogin walked to the barn still dark outside. You said you'd stay and you left cried Jean! I needed to see about Jed. You lied to me I hate you she slapped Constance's face. Constance grabbed Jeans hand I said I'd stay I just left after you were sleepin. Jean was angry and out of her head. She pulled Constance down Constance grabbed Jean's legs and Jean fell down. Jean was kickin and fightin like a wild animal. Jean snap out of it Constance pinned Jean down Jean was out of control so Constance slapped her face. Let me go said Jean! Not until you stop fightin said Constance. I'll stop I promise said Jean. Constance slowly let Jean get up. Jean was still cryin sorry Constance. Constance hugged Jean we need to pray for peace and strength so Constance prayed for Jean to have peace, comfort and strength. Amen.

Jean cried all day but she slept through the night. Astida carried her up to the loft where she could stay warmer. Constance stayed with Jed the weather was so freezin cold. Grandpa said way below zero and two feet of snow and ice. Jed was gettin his strength back. Zack wanted to go farther away than we thought would be safe and ice was fallin from the sky. Me and Astida found cover under trees then we made a run for home. Zack was too far away to hear us yell for him we waited as long as we could before we ran home. God brought you home safely to me Jed I love you, my heart breaks for Jean. These blizzards are so freezin cold and life threatin. Grandpa said not to trust the warm spells can turn into blizzards anytime with ice and deep snow. There's more warmth and food to eat when we stay and work together. I agree they snuggled and kissed.

Constance woke early to see about Jean. She was still sleepin. Constance let her sleep. She went to help Faith and Hope with breakfast. How's Jean? She's a bit better at least she's gettin some rest. We are in for a long winter said Faith. At least we are together, warm safe and food said Constance.

We can start plannin Christmas dinner and makin gifts for our children. I'll make Jean a little somethin special for Christmas said Faith. That's so sweet of you Faith. Jean needs us to help her survive her loss of Zack. Little Zeb walked in where's Daddy? Constance hugged Zeb he was almost three he was so close to his Daddy. Zeb your Daddy went somewhere real important he's in Heaven and he's watchin over you. I want to see Daddy? You will someday. Someday? Where's Momma? Zeb your Momma is here we can eat some breakfast together. Breakfast? For sure baby I'll fix yours right now you are my special boy! Zeb smiled and Constance went to get Zeb a royal breakfast. Baby Wayne, Bear and Nand came to sit by Zeb. They could see Zeb was down and out. Their presence cheered little Zeb. The boy's ate breakfast together in silence.

Jean walked in and hugged Zeb she needed to hold little Zeb for a while. Daddy's in Heaven Momma. Yes he is said Jean. When can we go to see Daddy? When God calls us. Oh said Zeb. Jean sat at the table holdin Zeb. Constance filled a plate of food for her. Jean was at least talkin and smilin some. Her heart was breakin for Zack. Zeb was the medicine Jean needed.

Chapter Sixteen

Low on Supplies

Christy's birthday. Everyone sang happy birthday to Christy. Constance made her a new dress and a baby doll. She hugged her doll. Hope made some dresses and tights for her. Faith gave her a gown and some socks. Grandpa made a rockin chair for Christy. Beth made socks and her favorite chocolate cake. Jean made a sweater all colors. Christy was all smiles! Jed gave her a sack of candy. Ogin gave her mittens. White Doe made her a warm hat. Grandma made her a shawl. They ate chocolate cake. Beth this is delicious said Constance.

The children played games all day with Summer always close by Christy was treated like a Queen! No one knew when Sutra or Nand's birthday was probably around spring Sutra would be five years old. Nand's birthday was about the same time Wayne's they would celebrate the boy's birthdays together.

Christmas was almost there. The women were so busy gettin gifts made and needed. Jean would be mournin for a long time. Grandma hugged Jean. She wasn't talkin much as she used to, Grandma understood love and hurt. Beth hugged Jean, so did Faith, Hope, White Doe and Ogin. Jean was loved by everyone who knew her, she was so attractive and sweet anyone who met her fell in love with her sweet ways. Little Zeb said I go play now Momma. Ok. Zeb baby you go play with your friends. They hugged Momma loves her baby boy. Love you Momma.

Jean slowly ate her breakfast. I miss Zack so. I'm so sorry Jean said Constance. I need somethin to do to take my mind off Zack. Would you like to cook or sew somethin? Yes I'll make somethin for Zeb for Christmas. Great we have material or yarn. He needs some overalls to wear he's growin so fast! Wonderful said Constance! I'll make some for

Wayne and Nand said Faith. So they got busy makin Zeb and boys some overalls for Christmas.

Plannin the meal. The soddy looked like Christmas Faith and Hope had decorated with red material. There wouldn't be a tree because of bein trapped in this winter. Gracy told all the children Christmas stories. Mostly about baby Jesus bein born to save us.

Christmas mornin Constance rose early to help cook by noon food was ready Jed said the blessin they ate. After dinner they exchanged gifts. What fun. Jed gave Constance a box she opened a beautiful locket oh thank you Jed she hugged him. Grandpa gave her a package. She opened a book of pictures of her Ma and Pa Grandpa and Grandma. Happy tears of joy.

The rest of the day was filled with love and laughter. Constance gave Jean a new dress. Jean was happier these days. They sang Christmas songs. Grandpa read Christmas story like he did in the past. He was the best at readin. Grandma was in good spirits.

Nand was runnin a fever he was burnin up, he was not feelin well for sure. Constance and Ogin put cold cloths on him to reduce his fever. He was so sweet and good natured. Sutra stayed by his side all day. She loved her baby brother.

Late at night Constance heard Nand throw up she went to see about him he threw up on the fire. Constance grabbed him he almost fell into the fire! She washed his face and rocked him back to sleep. She put Nand in bed next to Sutra, covered him up. She put some wood in fire then went back to her warm bed.

Next day Nand slept all day his fever had broken. Ogin said he do good he sleep.

Constance went to help in the kitchen. We need to ration our food more said Faith, we are low on meat and canned food. Alright we can make more gravy and beans said Constance. I'll make apple cobbler on Sunday said Hope. We have plenty of flour, coffee, cornmeal, turnips, some ham, beans and a few chickens, canned apple's and blackberries.

Almost March only broth for the winter now out of all food except water. Constance was weak tryin to keep her spirits up. As long as they stayed warm and drank broth they could survive the brutal winter. Everyone took more naps to save energy. Gettin weaker Constance drank her broth before she went to sleep. Prayin for them to be rescued. Jed was very weak from lack of food at least he was sleepin. Constance could see Grandma was slippin away thankful she was at peace and sleepin most of the time.

Bang Constance woke to a blast in the barn. Jed was too weak to go see so she kissed him and got her gun. Constance and Ogin with her knife slowly Constance drug her gun walked to barn with Summer. Oh thank God the barn door was open! She aimed her gun at a man with a beard was standin there. Sorry bout the dynamite blast. Only way to get in. Preacher ask me to see about you folks. How many people are alive in there? Not certain said Constance, we been trapped in all winter. Mind if I leave her in here? Martha's my best friend and he brought his mule into barn. Sure bring her in said Constance. We hungry said Ogin. Names Zeke he shook Constance and Ogin's hand. Let's go see about them other people. Constance and Ogin showed Zeke where everyone was. Zeke got a fire goin he gave Ogin a rabbit to cook. As soon as broth was ready Constance and Ogin drank a little and gave broth to all. Grandma drank just a tiny bit. Thank God everyone was alive just weak.

Zeke kept fire goin and Constance and Ogin kept broth hot. Jed was a little stronger. Zeke said he'd go see about Martha and other animals in the barn. Grandpa was gettin strength back so was Astida. Constance and Ogin were the strongest and able to take care of the others.

Gettin stronger they all held hands stood in a circle Grandpa said prayer thankin Good Lord for savin their lives.

Acknowlegements

I'd like to thank family and friends for all their love and support! Thank you Tracy Henry for typing my manuscript! Thank you fans on my facebook author page for your likes and support!

Printed in the United States
By Bookmasters